THE SILKEN SECRET

THE
SILKEN
SECRET

by GEOFFREY TREASE

NEW YORK • THE VANGUARD PRESS

CONTENTS

THE SILKEN SECRET

1. Sixpence From a Stranger

"Arlington!"

The voice was soft, even silky, but full of danger.

Of the sixty-three pens busily scratching in the long schoolroom sixty-two fell silent. Only Dick Arlington went on writing, hunched over his ancient desk.

His thoughts were far away. Mechanically, with all the right loops and flourishes, his pen moved across the page, copying the *Rules of Civility and Decent Behavior in Company and Conversation*. There were altogether one hundred and ten of them, but he was now

9

within sight of the last: *"Labor to keep alive in your Breast that little Spark of Celestial Fire called Conscience."*

"Arlington!"

The assistant raised his voice. He stepped forward and squinted down the gangway between the desks. When the headmaster was present, Mr. Coope was apt to mince and cringe; when left in charge, as now, he straightened his lanky figure and stuck out his waistcoat, all stained and dusty with spilled snuff. Somehow Mr. Coope could never inspire respect, but he knew very well how to instill fear.

"Sir?"

Dick Arlington raised his long brown head with a twitching movement as of one suddenly awakened. With obvious difficulty he brought himself back to the paneled walls and handsome molded ceiling of Abbotsbridge Grammar School. Slowly his dark eyes focused on the assistant, glowering down at him from under the balustraded gallery. Rather late in the day, he remembered to stand up.

"Yes, sir—you, sir!" Mr. Coope's tongue bit like a horsewhip. "Come up here, sir." Dick laid down his pen and obeyed, his heavy country shoes clumping over the wooden floor. "You have an object bulging out your pocket, boy. Remove it."

"Yes, sir."

Something glinted in the sunlight. There was a gasp from the smallest boys in the front rows. Even Mr. Coope drew in his breath with a sharp little hiss.

A pistol. If the boy had actually fired it, he could

hardly have produced a stronger effect. Every pen remained motionless. The *Rules of Civility and Decent
Behavior* were forgotten. There was a rustle of whispers.

"The fool! Bringing a pistol in here!"

"Coope will flog him for sure."

"Maybe he won't. Dick's just over the smallpox."

"Coope won't care."

"Neither will Dick. It'll take more than Coope to
make *him* squeal."

Ten seconds had passed without a word spoken on
the platform. It was true: Mr. Coope had never found
Arlington a very satisfactory victim. The severest flog-
ging never won more than a low grunt from his set lips.
"That boy is like my Greek dictionary," the headmaster, Dr. Payton, had once remarked. "He not only
contains within himself a fair quantity of that language
—I fancy he is strongly bound in leather as well."

Mr. Coope glanced uneasily at the weapon on the
desk. It was an ordinary flintlock pistol, the kind carried
by army officers. Then his gaze swept back to the waiting boy. Arlington was unusually pale. Was he for once
afraid? But no, those brown eyes were steady, the chin
uptilted and defiant. For the first time Mr. Coope saw
the peppering of fresh pockmarks—faint, but sufficient
to remind him that the boy had just recovered from
smallpox. Irritably, Mr. Coope concluded that this was
the only reason for Arlington's pallor. Never mind, if
he was well enough to return to school, he was well
enough to be whipped.

"A pistol!" said the assistant. "Loaded?"

"Oh, *no*, sir. Of course not, sir."

Mr. Coope took the weapon in his hand with more confidence. "Intolerable behavior! To introduce a fire-arm into class!" He began to work up his indignation. "Upon my word, boy, you seem to have no notion——"

"Excuse me, sir——"

"No doubt you are well primed with some lying excuse. I know your sort. Well?"

The boy hesitated. The muscles in his throat worked as he swallowed.

"Well? Do your powers of invention for once desert you? Have you nothing to say?"

A moment's silence. Then came Arlington's voice, low but clear. "No, sir."

"Very well." Mr. Coope reached for the birch, then murmured thoughtfully: "No—I think not." He raised his voice. "Hemingway!"

"Yessir?" A small boy bobbed up.

"Fetch me my dogwhip. You will find it——" Mr. Coope hesitated as a murmur of protest rolled toward him from the back of the hall. "Silence!" he snarled. Then, bending toward Hemingway, he resumed: "You will find the whip——"

"One moment, Mr. Coope, if you please." The head-master's voice rang out from the doorway.

"Oh—by all means, Dr. Payton."

Dr. Payton marched down the gangway like a little general, his hat set very squarely on his short black peri-wig and the skirts of his blue coat slanting wide and stiff behind him. His eyes fell on the pistol.

"In heaven's name, Arlington, what's this?"

"Only an old pistol, sir."

"I can see that. What's it doing here?"

"I have just confiscated it, Dr. Payton," said the assistant smugly, "and was about to deal with the culprit."

"So I gathered." Short as he was, the headmaster seemed to overtop his assistant. "You may sit down, Hemingway, you will not be needed. Mr. Coope had forgotten, of course, that Arlington has been very ill. I will deal with the boy myself, Mr. Coope—more suitably."

"By all means, Dr. Payton."

The headmaster fixed the whole school with his gaze. "It is strictly against the rules to bring any dangerous object into class," he said severely. "You all know that. Arlington is not a complete fool. Therefore, it may be that Arlington had a reason." He paused.

"Yes, sir. I had—" For the first time the boy's voice shook a little. He gulped. "Nowhere else to keep it, sir."

Mr. Coope snorted, but Dr. Payton quelled him with a look. "Was it your father's pistol, my boy?"

"Yes, sir, he had it at the Battle of Blenheim. Afterward my mother . . . kept it for me. And now—"

"Take it back," said the headmaster gently. He pulled out his watch and studied it, shooting back his frilled cuff with a dignified gesture. "It wants only two minutes to eleven o'clock. The school is dismissed."

Mr. Coope leaned forward, licking his lips anxiously. "You will not forget, Dr. Payton, this boy Arlington—"

"Thank you, Mr. Coope, I shall deal with him myself—suitably. Arlington, you will wash your hands and present yourself at my front door in precisely five minutes. You will be having dinner with me."

Dick Arlington did not mind having dinner with the headmaster. Dr. Payton was all right. Mrs. Payton did not count. The only alarming features presented by the invitation were those of Dr. Payton's daughters, six in number, various in age, size, and shape, who ranged themselves down both sides of the table and eyed any young male guest as though they would far rather devour him than the beef and pudding in front of them. However, Dick emerged from this ordeal without so much as a tooth mark, and, dinner over, was swept off into the headmaster's study. Here he was amused to see that a book open on the table was a gruesome-looking murder story, *The Apprentice Who Murdered His Mistress*.

Hastily covering this with a heavy volume of sermons, Dr. Payton took a pinch of snuff, waved Dick to a chair, and settled himself in his own. "Well, my boy, what's to be done?"

"You mean the pistol, sir?"

"No, no, no. I can guess why you brought it to school, and didn't want to say in front of all the boys."

"You see, it's *my* pistol, sir. But if I'd left it in the cottage they'd have taken it with all Mother's things. They say Mother owed a great many bills. She got behindhand, with our both being ill—it wasn't her fault, sir—"

"I know, my boy. I knew the bailiff's men were moving in today."

"Mrs. Williams said—she's the woman next door who's looking after me—she said I'd better keep the pistol in my pocket, as it was mine, or they'd sell it with the rest. It's the only thing of my father's that I have left, sir."

It was also, though Dick did not mention it, the only thing he had left in the world at all, barring what he stood up in, a spare shirt and change of underclothes.

Dr. Payton sighed. "Let me see. Blenheim was fought in 1704. You're scarcely fourteen now . . . you don't remember you father, do you?"

"Dimly, sir. Mostly his red coat, and his sword. The sword never came back." Dick looked at his shoe buckles and remembered, just in time, that he must not kick the legs of Dr. Payton's table.

"I've been talking to the Vicar." Dr. Payton took another pinch of snuff. "It seems that the Squire—the *old* Squire, I should say—said your mother was to have the cottage as long as she lived. And the present Squire always honored that promise, though he had never known your father."

"Yes, sir."

"Now—er—the situation is altered."

"Mother's dead," said Dick gruffly.

"Precisely. And even if you were allowed to keep the cottage, a boy of your age could not live by himself."

"There isn't any money, sir. It was always very hard to manage. Mother stopped her dressmaking when she had to nurse me, and then she got the smallpox herself. . . ."

"Yes. Well, you must try to forget what you have

been through. Think of the future. How and where are you to live?"

"I'll be all right, sir. I haven't had time to make any plans yet."

"The Vicar and I have made plans for you," Dr. Payton informed him kindly, "since you have no relatives. Next year you'll be fifteen, old enough to go up to Oxford as originally expected—"

"Oxford, sir? But I haven't a penny!"

"The school has its own close scholarships to Cardigan College. You could eke out the money as other poor scholars have to do—waiting on the young gentlemen who are better off."

Dick wrinkled his nose distastefully. The idea of earning his living as servant to other boys—cleaning their boots, making their fires, and fetching their meals from the college kitchen—did not greatly appeal to him.

"Till then," went on the headmaster, clasping his hands comfortably over his long waistcoat, "we must find you cheap but decent lodgings."

"Who is to pay, sir?"

"There will be no great difficulty there, I fancy. I shall make my contribution. Several other gentlemen will help. And the Vicar thinks that a pound or two may be gotten from Alderman Mayott's Charity."

The last word stung Dick as Mr. Coope's whip could never have done. "I'm sorry, sir," he burst out, "but that's the one thing I don't want! Charity!"

Dr. Payton frowned. "Be reasonable, boy, you can't help yourself."

It was an unfortunate remark. To Dick it rang like

a challenge. So he could not help himself? They should see.

For the next ten minutes the discussion was heated. Dr. Payton pointed out that no one could live on air, least of all a growing boy, and that for Dick to start work at once would be a waste of the brains God had given him. What work was there for him in Abbotsbridge? Was he to go as potboy in an alehouse, or to sweep stables, or to labor for a farmer?

In the end, the headmaster flung off his wig in a tantrum and mopped his glistening skull with a large white handkerchief. The market clock chimed a quarter past twelve. At one they must both be back in school, and he had been looking forward to an after-dinner doze before then.

"You're a pigheaded youth, Arlington," he said tartly. "I can't bandy words with you all day. Go along now, think matters over, and perhaps you will see reason."

"Yes, sir. And—thank you very much for the dinner, sir."

Dick bowed himself out, picked up his hat, and stepped from the cool, white-paneled hall into the noonday glare of the market place. And there he saw not reason but, standing in the black shadow of the old Abbey Gateway, the strange figure who was to twist the whole direction of his life.

No other figure stirred in the drowsy sunshine.

The square lay empty, one side enclosed by the gabled frontage of the Antelope and another by the Town Hall, graceful and lofty on its pillars. To the left, the street ran down past the Crown and Thistle, and over the long bridge across the Thames. To the right, spanning a quiet lane, was the ancient gatehouse, and under its vaulted archway stood the stranger.

He was a tall, rawboned man of doubtful age, with a sharp questing nose, a nutcracker jaw, and big teeth, like a horse's, ranged under a remarkably long upper lip. His eyes were green, shrewd, and humorous, with sandy brows bent comically above them. Green, too, was his coat, a kind of bottle green. As he stepped forward into the full sunlight, cane in one hand, three-cornered hat in the other, so as not to disarrange his chestnut wig, he was most noticeably bowlegged.

"One moment, me boy." He raised his cane and beckoned.

An Irishman, Dick decided from his accent. He walked over with a pleasant twinge of curiosity. Strangers were few in Abbotsbridge.

The outside world had always fascinated him. Watching the coaches rumble out of the town, he had often longed to follow them. Splashing in the Thames with his friends, he had often stopped to stare after the barges, hauling heavy goods between Oxford and London, and had ached to follow the river down to where it met gulls and masted ships and the open sea. The Irishman, standing there like a huge bluebottle, was a figure from that interesting outer world.

"Yes, sir?"

"Ye look an honest boy. Ye look an intelligent boy." The Irishman thrust his hand into his breeches pocket. "Would ye care to earn sixpence?"

"Yes, sir. But—" His grin faded as a thought struck him. "I have to be back in school by one o'clock."

"Never fear, me boy. What I'm askin' ye will take only a few minnuts. First—" The stranger looked down and fixed him with a keen stare. "Is there a lady in this town o' the name o' Smith?"

"Oh, yes, sir! There's Mrs. Smith at the malthouse, and young Mrs. Smith, the curate's wife, and old Lizzie Smith down at the almshouses, and—which Mrs. Smith do you mean, sir?"

"I have not the least idea, me boy, but 'tis of no consequence at all. Now I'll be telling ye what ye have to do."

"Yes, sir?"

"Ye're to walk down this street as far as the bridge an' stay there till—" the Irishman twisted his head to peer up at the market clock—"till that clock chimes the quarter to the hour. Then run to the Antelope yonder. Fast as ye can, mind. Ye should be quite breathless, if ye're earning ye sixpence. Just keep enough breath for ye message."

"But—" Dick gaped. "If it's urgent, wouldn't it be more sensible to take it now?"

The Irishman smiled pityingly. "An' what would be the use of taking a message *now* to a gentleman, who, at this moment, as I happen to know for a positive fact, is not there at all?"

"Beg your pardon, sir!" Dick felt a little crushed. "What is the message, please?"

" 'Tis just this, and ye must deliver it exactly, mind— not a word less or more. 'Mrs. Smith is took very bad, and will ye please to come at once, because she says there's no other doctor in the wide world can save her?' Can ye remember that, me boy?"

"Oh, yes, sir." Dick repeated the message.

"An' don't be askin' me *which* Mrs. Smith. The doctor'll know well enough."

"And, please, sir, what is the name of the doctor?"

"Dr. O'Flynn."

There was no such doctor in Abbotsbridge. "Oh—" the words slipped out without any intention of rudeness—"*another* Irishman?"

"He *is* Irish," said the stranger sternly, "an' with the best degrees of Trinity College, Dublin, an' of Leyden University in Holland. If ye were to ask for the *great* Dr. O'Flynn, there would be no manner of harm in it at all." He pulled out a sixpence, eyed it with a lingering expression, and dropped it into Dick's hand. "Ye'll be wonderin' at me trustin' ye," he said, "an' you a strange boy that I've never clapped eyes on before?"

"No, sir," said Dick frankly. He would never have thought of taking the sixpence and *not* delivering the message.

"Ye see, I summed ye up as honest the minnut I saw ye. Sum a man up I can, in the twinklin' of an eye, an' a great gift it is, very necessary in my profession. Now be off with ye, me boy, for the clock's creepin' round to the half-hour."

Dick strolled down the hill and lolled on the bridge, watching the swans. Which Mrs. Smith was so ill? How had the message come into the hands of the Irishman, a stranger in the town? Why must Dick himself arrive

breathless, just after a quarter to one? At least the puzzle served to take his mind off his own worries.

Mrs. Smith (whoever she was) must have heard that
the famous doctor was lodging at the Antelope. Stricken
with a sudden illness, she had sent an urgent appeal for
help. What more natural than that this message should
first come, by mistake, to another Irishman? And that
he, having discovered that Dr. O'Flynn would not return until a quarter to one, should tip a boy to deliver
it?

As for the business of running all the way and arriving
breathless, that (Dick supposed, with a smile) was just
an artistic touch, to impress on Dr. O'Flynn that the
case was urgent. Fair enough. Poor Mrs. Smith had
been waiting long enough for medical attention.

He looked at the sixpence, idly spelling out the Latin
around the Queen's head. *Anne, by the grace of God.
. . .* Was the coin an omen? He had earned some
money within a few minutes of leaving the headmaster.
He sighed. Such chances did not come every day.

The clock startled him by its sudden chime. He
jumped up and began to run. The street was awakening
again after the dinner hour. Some of the boys were
drifting back in twos and threes, others were already
playing with a ball in the yard.

"What's the hurry, Dick?" one of them called.

"Can't stop now!" he panted.

He was determined to earn that sixpence. He clat-
tered across the square, his nailed shoes striking sparks
from the cobbles. In the shadowy entrance to the inn he
caromed against the landlord.

"Here, lad, steady! What do *you* want?"

"I've a message for Dr. O'Flynn. The great Dr. O'Flynn," Dick added conscientiously.

"Oh, he's great, is he?" It was evidently news to the landlord. "He's a great talker, that I *do* know." He jerked his thumb toward a doorway on the left. "In there, lad."

Dick went in. The room was hazy with tobacco smoke, and crowded with men. He stopped on the threshold, a little shy. An aproned valet, his hands bunching several tankards each, wheeled around and bent an inquiring head. "What is it, sir?"

"An urgent message for Dr. O'Flynn, if he's here." Dick repeated it as he had been told. Without a moment's hesitation the servant turned and bellowed through the smoke-hung room.

"Dr. O'Flynn? If you please, sir!"

"Here!" The response came, faint through the hubbub, from a busy group in the far corner.

"Urgent message, Doctor," the servant bawled. Instantly the other voices were stilled. Heads turned with interest. "Mrs. Smith is took very bad. Will you please come at once? She says you're the only doctor in the world can save her!"

This announcement had all the effect that anyone could have desired. Eyes opened wider. Snuffboxes stayed poised in midair. One elegant gentleman raised an eyeglass to survey the scene.

Dick waited to make sure that his message had been received, and because he was curious to see the famous doctor. He was quite unprepared for what happened next.

The group in the far corner was breaking up, with a chorus of compliments and apologies, to let the doctor out. And now, as the chairs scraped back to right and left, a tall figure sailed majestically through the tobacco haze.

It was the man who had given him the sixpence, not half an hour before.

Dick's jaw dropped. As the stranger drew near, he stammered: "P-please, sir—but—Dr. O'Flynn?"

"*I* am Dr. O'Flynn, very much at ye service, and the service of all who are afflicted." It was the same Irish brogue, but the tone was formal and magnificent, the tone of a man who had never seen him before.

"But—"

The Irishman's hand fell on his shoulder and spun him around. "Yes, yes, me boy, tell me the symptoms as we go. That poor sufferin' woman must not be kept waitin' a minnut longer."

Dick found himself outside. Still keeping a firm grip on his shoulder, the Irishman propelled him rapidly around the nearest corner, and down one of the back streets.

"I—I don't understand, sir—"

"How should ye, me boy, though 'tis a smart intelligent boy ye are, to be sure? The medical profession has its own mysteries, an' 'tis not for the uninstructed to be pryin' into them." He let go Dick's shoulder. "Ye've earned ye sixpence, me boy, an' if ye'd like to earn another, later on, I might be able to put ye in the way of it. Me own boy, that I had, quit me at the last town—not a word o' warnin' either—and 'tis vastly inconvenienced I am."

In the distance the school bell began to clang, recalling Dick to the world where he belonged. "I must go, sir. There's the bell for school. And," he added, utterly confused, "you'll be wanting to hurry on to Mrs. Smith's."

Dr. O'Flynn smiled down at him and nodded. "Ay, to be sure, to be sure. For one minnut I'd forgotten the poor lady. 'Twould never do to let Mrs. Smith die on us. She's far too useful, dear soul."

He strode away, important and even, despite his bowlegs, magnificent. Dick stared after him for a few moments, puzzled and fascinated. Then, as the bell faltered and stopped, he turned and ran.

2. The London Coach

Sixpence is sixpence.

That fact had been firmly impressed upon Dick ever since he could remember.

Life had been hard for his mother, sewing and dressmaking, sometimes in their own small cottage, sometimes in the big houses of the gentry. But never had he realized the importance of money so keenly as during the last month. He had seen the cottage stripped of its shabby but friendly furniture to pay for his mother's funeral and debts. He was living now on the kindness of neighbors as poor as himself, and, if the Vicar and Dr. Payton had their way, he would continue to live on charity for the next year.

He came out of school at five o'clock with one thought: if there were any more sixpences to be earned from Dr. O'Flynn, he was going to earn them, and hand them straight to Mrs. Williams, toward his board.

He went across to the Antelope. The landlord was standing in the doorway. "Not *another* of you for Dr. O'Flynn?" he said. "They've been coming all afternoon. If there's been one, there's been a dozen. The word's got around the town, you see."

"I—I suppose he's a very famous doctor?"

"I should say he is!" The landlord's respect for Dr. O'Flynn had grown considerably during the afternoon. "It's real luck for Abbotsbridge, the doctor passing through like this. May make all the difference to some poor souls."

"I hope so," said Dick sincerely. A thought stabbed him: if only Dr. O'Flynn had come a week or two sooner, his mother might have been saved. . . . But it was no use brooding. "Do you know when he'll be back, please?" he asked.

"Couldn't say—or how long he'll stop when he is. He doesn't spare himself, I'll say that for the gentleman. It's in and out again, straightway, if he hears there's another patient waiting. Where is he wanted now, lad?"

"Oh, it isn't for a patient," Dick explained awkwardly. "I—I just wanted to see him. He told me I could come."

The landlord shrugged his shoulders. "You might catch him at his supper, but there's no telling when that'll be—"

Dick was turning away, disappointed, when the gaunt

figure of the Irishman came striding across the cobbles. A red-cheeked maidservant trotted anxiously at his heels, but he seemed unaware of her existence until he reached the door, when he swung around and said: "Ye must wait here for the physic, me dear." She bobbed respectfully, too breathless for speech.

The landlord and Dick had stepped aside. Dr. O'Flynn cast a quick glance to left and right. To the landlord he said: "Have ye shifted me bags?" The landlord bowed. "Yes, Doctor, and I trust you'll be more comfortable in your new room." The shrewd green eyes turned upon Dick. "Ah, me boy, come along in for a minnut." They went inside together and up the stairs.

The bedroom doors all carried names—the Paragon, the Globe, the Star. Dr. O'Flynn paused outside the Moon.

"This is it, I'm thinkin'." He chuckled. "Mine host suddenly decided, this afternoon, I must have one o' the better bedrooms." He led the way in. "Ay, there are me bags." He crossed to a couple of well-worn leather bags by the four-poster bed, opened one, and produced a box of pills. "Will ye run down and give these to the maidservant?" he asked. "Then come back here."

"Yes, Doctor." Dick departed on willing feet. When he came back the Irishman had flung off his wig, kicked aside his shoes, and sunk into a chair.

"What a day, me young friend! 'Tis an extraordinary unhealthy town ye live in. What's ye name, eh?"

"Dick. Dick Arlington, Doctor."

"Well, young Dick, ye did the trick." He chuckled at his own rhyme. "Ye certainly brought me luck."

"I—I don't understand, Doctor. And I'm still puzzled about that message from Mrs. Smith."

"Never worry ye head over that, me boy." The Irishman winked. "No harm in it at all. A stratagem, ye might say."

Dick tried to look shocked, but there was something infectious about the doctor's smile. "You mean, there wasn't really any Mrs. Smith who was ill?"

"If there was, me boy, she's made no call on me professional services. But she must be almost the only invalid in Abbotsbridge that hasn't." He thrust his hands into his breeches pockets and clinked their contents with satisfaction. "I've brought new hope, Dick, where there was only despair," he went on solemnly. "And that's a very great thing, ye know; a very great thing."

"Yes, Doctor."

"But how else could those poor souls have learned there was a strange physician passing through their town? Was I to march the streets beatin' a drum?" The green eyes fixed Dick with an earnest gaze. "Ye can tell yeself this, Dick Arlington: that innocent deception, in which ye assisted me, may have saved long months of agony, years maybe of sad, body-wastin' decline, or even—who can say?—the sudden stroke of remorseless Death himself."

"Yes, Doctor."

There was a spellbinding power in the Irishman's eloquence. Dick's hesitation faded. It was a privilege to have helped him in his noble work.

"Would ye like to earn another sixpence?" the doctor

demanded. " 'Tis no message-runnin', this time. 'Tis only to deliver a few bottles o' physic and suchlike around the town."

"I'd be glad to do that, Doctor."

For the next hour Dick trudged around, delivering bottles of medicine, pots of ointment, powders, and pills. When he returned, the doctor was just sitting down to a supper of veal cutlets, pigeons, and cheese. A tankard of ale stood at hand.

"Good boy! I can see ye've wasted no time." He pulled out a handful of silver, selected a sixpence, rejected it, and, after an interval of anxious consideration (no less anxious for Dick), presented him with a shilling.

"Oh! Thank you very much, Doctor!"

"Truth to tell, me boy, ye came in most handy. Me regular lad left me in the lurch, he did—a lad, mark ye, that I'd trained this past twelvemonth, and looked after the way he was me own son. Then, without a word of warning, off he goes! I tell ye," said the Irishman sadly, taking a long pull at his ale, "it destroys a man's faith in human nature entirely, so it does."

"Will you be here for long, Doctor?"

"Only tomorrow, me boy."

"Oh . . . I see." Hope shrank.

"I'm called back to London, ye see—a certain great nobleman, whose name I am not at liberty to mention —" The Irishman broke off to glance cautiously round the dining room, but seemed more disappointed than relieved to find that they were alone. "His Grace is travelin' down from the North to consult me. 'Tis a desperate case. But the patient cannot reach town for another two days, so there is no sense in hurryin' meself."

"I suppose you'll engage another boy when you get to London?"

Dick's voice was wistful. How interesting to work for Dr. O'Flynn, traveling the length and breadth of Britain, learning the secrets of the medical profession, entering great houses, and seeing illustrious patients! London, Dublin, Bath, York, Oxford, Cambridge, Bristol, Norwich . . . one might see all these, and a hundred other places.

Dr. O'Flynn caught that wistfulness and gave him a keen look. "No doubt," he said, helping himself to another cutlet. "There's many a father in the city—substantial merchants, ay, and gentry too—would think it a favor to 'prentice his son to Dr. Nathaniel O'Flynn. But I'll not take just any boy, Dick, not though his dad were Lord Mayor. No scatterbrained rapscallion for me! 'Tis a privilege to be admitted into the mysteries of medicine." He paused. "And what is *your* father, me boy?"

Dick explained. The doctor shook his head sadly and took some pigeon. " 'Tis a poor prospect for ye, Dick. An orphan, and no inheritance at all. Nobody even to 'prentice ye in an honest trade."

Dick was by now faint with hunger. But he was not going to leave Dr. O'Flynn now until he had forced himself to ask the question uppermost in his mind.

"You wouldn't let me come and work for you, Doctor?"

An expression of blank amazement flooded across the Irishman's bony face. He stared up at the waiting boy. Dick flushed, and wished that the substantial floor boards of the Antelope dining room would part and swallow him.

"That," said Dr. O'Flynn slowly and gravely, "is a most—a *most* extraordinary—suggestion. It can only be excused on the grounds of extreme youth an' ignorance. Ye've just told me ye haven't a penny in the world—"

"I *am* sorry, Doctor," Dick mumbled.

"There, there," Dr. O'Flynn reassured him. "Ye were not to know. Besides—" he snapped his long fingers— "Nathaniel O'Flynn doesn't care *that* for all the money-bags in London. D'ye know any Latin?"

"Oh, yes, Doctor! I've done Caesar, Virgil, Horace, Ovid, Cicero, Propertius—"

"Stop, stop, me boy! That's Latin enough to cure any stomach-ache. Dick Arlington, I like ye face. Maybe I've told ye, I can sum up people in a twinkling? Good. Ye have no money to pay a premium. No matter. Ye dad died a hero's death at Blenheim. The nation owes him a debt, and O'Flynn's the man to pay it. Dick, me boy," he announced, raising his tankard with a splendid gesture, "ye shall take the coach to London with me—and good luck to the both of us!"

It was not quite as simple as that.

Mrs. Williams made no great objection when Dick told her. She was a kindly soul, and saw that a complete change might be the best thing for a boy who had just lost everything. But Dr. Payton was a harder nut to crack.

"Who is this Dr. O'Flynn?" he demanded. "Yes, yes, of course I've *heard* of him. I hear his name all over town. But I had never heard it before yesterday evening. What do we know of his character? All manner of people call themselves doctors, and as often as not they're just ignorant quacks and pretenders."

The headmaster was vexed. Dick was not a brilliant scholar, but he had always been one of the better boys. Dr. Payton had looked forward to sending him on to Oxford, and, during the past week, he had taken a good deal of trouble finding ways for Dick to finish his school career.

The more suspicious Dr. Payton became, the more stubbornly Dick clung to his new plan. He had set his heart on going with Dr. O'Flynn. In that way he would start at once to earn his living and he would be seeing the world at the same time.

"I don't *want* to go to college now," he protested.

"And why not, pray?"

"College is all right for gentlemen, with money and prospects afterwards. Oh, I know, sir, I could work my way through Oxford somehow, but what should I be fit for at the end? Only a parson, or a schoolmaster—"

Dick stopped, horrified, and clapped his hand over his mouth, but too late. His last remark, thrown out in the heat of the moment, did nothing to cool the air.

But Dr. Payton was a fair-minded little man, and, though he snorted angrily enough, he was determined to keep his temper and do all he could to save the boy from his own folly.

"I am not your guardian—you do not appear to possess one—but I know that if your poor mother had lived she would have consulted me. We should both have wanted to know more about this Dr. O'Flynn—"

"Would it help, sir, if I could get him to come and see you?"

"*If* you could," said Dr. Payton darkly. "But if I am any judge, this gentleman will steer clear of me—and of anybody else likely to ask awkward questions. His one wish is to leave Abbotsbridge tomorrow morning, with a cheap assistant—"

He was interrupted by a tap on the study door. One of the Payton girls poked her head around and announced: "A gentleman to see you, Father—Dr. O'Flynn!"

The Irishman came in with a flourish. The headmaster started up like a fighting cock prepared for battle.

"Ye servant, sir," said the Irishman pleasantly.

"This is a most welcome surprise, Doctor. I had not expected this honor. Dick, a chair for Dr. O'Flynn."

The Irishman handed Dick his hat and cane with an elegant gesture. "Ye'll guess, sir, 'tis about the boy."

"Indeed?" Dr. Payton was wary. "He has told me . . . *something* . . . about you and your proposal."

"Then that'll save us time, Dr. Payton. For there's one or two questions I have to ask ye."

"Questions?" echoed the headmaster. "You come

here to ask *me* questions?" He puffed out his cheeks.
"I must know something about any lad I take into
me service. 'Tis not just anybody I would be picking up.
No offense, Dick," O'Flynn added with a disarming
smile. "Maybe, with Dr. Payton's kind permission, ye'd
go outside, so we could talk more freely?"

"Yes, yes, wait in the hall," said Dr. Payton hastily.
He was not used to hearing anyone else issue orders in
his own study.

Dick went out. The last words he caught before the
door closed were: "Now, Dr. Payton, is the boy well
grounded in his Latin?"

He sat down in the hall to wait with what patience
he could muster. The slow minutes ticked by. Dr. Payton had one of the new-fangled grandfather clocks which
King William had brought in from Holland. Dick
watched the swinging pendulum until he was almost
mesmerized.

Suppose, after all, Dr. O'Flynn refused to take him?
Suppose he was not satisfied with Dick's character or
offended by Dr. Payton's suspicious manner?

Five minutes passed. Ten. Fifteen. Twenty.

The door opened. He heard genial voices. "Mark
me words, sir," the Irishman was saying, "that is the seat
of the trouble. I'll send ye round a bottle tonight.
Take it before ye sleep, sir, and then three times
daily."

Dr. Payton appeared, holding open the door. "I am
vastly obliged, Doctor."

"Delighted to be of service, sir."

"Then—good day to you, Dr. O'Flynn."

"Ye servant, Dr. Payton!"

After an exchange of bows at the front door, the headmaster closed it behind his visitor. He seemed surprised to find Dick still waiting in the hall.

"Please, sir—is everything all right, sir?"

"All right? Why, of course, my boy, of course! I have every confidence in Dr. O'Flynn. You could not be in better hands. By the way—" Dr. Payton coughed a little shamefacedly—"Dr. O'Flynn has promised to send me a bottle of cordial. See that he doesn't forget."

"He won't, sir," Dick promised delightedly. "I'll bring it myself, sir, when I come to say good-by."

Meanwhile, as Dr. O'Flynn walked away, an urchin rushed around the corner and almost collided with him. Recovering his balance, the child was reaching for the door knocker to give a thunderous rat-tat when a thought struck him and he stammered breathlessly:

"Beg pardon, sir—are *you* the—the great Dr. O'Flynn? Because Mrs. Smith is took bad, and says there isn't another doctor in the wide world—"

"Don't be a fool," said the Irishman roughly, showing his big horse teeth. "Ye're too late, ye idle young scamp. But no matter. I managed well enough without ye!"

The market clock was striking six, next morning, when Dr. O'Flynn seated himself in the coach and Dick scrambled aloft, where the humbler sort of passenger belonged. Dr. Payton bowed from his doorway and waved his hat, before going in to morning school. The ostlers stood back, the horses started forward, and away

they went, down the hill and over the bridge. The country rose to meet them—green and snowy-white and
butter-gold, the air throbbing with bird song, and
honeysweet with the scents of May.

Dick turned his head. Abbotsbridge was slipping
behind, already half-blotted by the trees—just a cluster
of roofs crowned by the Town Hall weathercock and
St. Helen's spire. His lips moved silently. Good-by,
Abbotsbridge . . . London tonight!

It was nearly sixty miles, but, the guard assured Dick
proudly, the Abbotsbridge Flyer was one of the fastest
services on the road.

"Have you ever been stopped?" Dick inquired.

"Stopped? By the gentlemen o' the road, ye mean?
Nay, touch wood, I've never been unlucky that way."

"I've got a pistol," Dick confided, and produced it.

"Loaded?" asked the guard nervously.

"No—but a highwayman wouldn't *know* that. I could
point it."

"Just a moment, young 'un. That's a very fine
weapon, that is." The guard satisfied himself that it
was not loaded, and gave it back. "Certainly you could
point it, point it as much as you like. Any highwayman
would think again if he saw a pistol like that."

"Well," said Dick with satisfaction, slipping it away
again, "just because you've never been held up yet
doesn't mean you won't be today. In fact, it's all the
more likely you will be. Dr. Payton explained it all to
us. By the law of mathematical probability—"

"Hold on," objected the guard, "if this here coach is

held up it won't be accordin' to any law, it'll be very much *against* the law!"

Meanwhile the Abbotsbridge Flyer bowled eastward, mile by mile, hour by hour, through the summer day. Dr. O'Flynn had a friendly word for him at each stage where the horses were changed. The Irishman was getting along famously with his fellow passengers inside, and, when the coach halted for dinner, Dick had to get down one of the bags containing the medicines.

And so, early in the evening, they reached the outskirts of London. Through the village of Kensington they rumbled—Dick's eyes straining for a glimpse of Queen Anne's palace—and on down Piccadilly, past the windmill and the haymarket, to Charing Cross and the busy streets of which he had dreamed.

3. Doctor's Boy

Dusk was already settling over London as the coach
came to a standstill. Dick had a confused impression of
burly men pressing their services as coachmen and chairmen; and of linkboys, with twinkling lanterns, offering
to light the way through the darkening streets. In the
background loomed tall houses, patched with the yellow
squares of big casement windows, candlelit.

Their fellow passengers melted away. The Abbotsbridge Flyer wheeled under an arch and vanished.

"Have we far to go, Doctor?" Dick inquired.

"Not if our luck is in. We should be able to find a decent lodging hereabouts."

38

"Oh." Dick's heart sank. He was tired and hungry.

" 'Tis some time since I left town, ye see, and I gave up me old lodgin', not knowin' just when I'd be back."

"But they'd know you there, wouldn't they?"

"H'm. . . . True enough, me boy. They'll not have forgotten me." Dr. O'Flynn's tone was doubtful, as if this was not entirely an advantage. "But I'm minded to make a change. Me old lodgin' was not proper at all for a gentleman. The world judges a man by appearances."

They found lodgings, after a great deal of haggling, in a courtyard opening, by a narrow slit of an alley, off Fleet Street. Dick was too tired to notice much that night; but the next morning, when he surveyed the rooms and the whole dingy surroundings of Mercers Court, he could not help wondering what the doctor's previous quarters had been like, if these were an improvement.

They had three rooms on the second floor—a sitting room and bedroom for the doctor, and an airless little cubbyhole where Dick slept and the medicines were stored.

" 'Tis somewhat musty, maybe," the Irishman admitted, poking his long nose through the doorway, "but the fine healthy smell o' physic will soon kill that. I always mix me own physic. These apothecary fellows are half of 'em rogues."

"Will you teach *me* how to mix medicines, Doctor?"

"Ye shall have a full an' proper trainin' in every branch o' the medical art. But one thing at a time, me boy."

The first thing, it appeared, was to fetch some more

pots and bottles. "Ye can't miss the place," Dr. O'Flynn assured him, "but hold hard to ye money. And ye can warn that old scoundrel Joey Rookman that ye master knows well what makes a shillingsworth, and if he gives ye any less he'll be hearing from *me*."

Dick was glad to get out of the fusty house and its dark courtyard, and face the pure morning sun shining along Fleet Street. It was a wide road, crowded with hackney coaches and carts, with here and there a horseman, or a sedan chair. Foot passengers had to keep inside the posts lining either side, if they did not wish to be knocked down.

Joey Rookman was a sly, greasy little person, though —as Dick realized—it would have been hard to keep clean in such a business, which seemed to consist mainly of picking over an extraordinary mound of rubbish in a dark and smelly shed.

"Here y' are, lad," he said, pushing over a sack. "Mind, now, and don't smash 'em. There was none broken when they went in, yer saw for yerself."

"Thank you." Dick swung the sack gingerly over his shoulder, and went rattling and clinking back to Mercers Court.

This was not quite the kind of work he had pictured for himself as Dr. O'Flynn's apprentice, but it would be quite different later in the day when he spruced himself up and attended the doctor to the house of the sick nobleman.

When he got back he found that a fire had been lit in the doctor's bedroom, and that the Irishman had borrowed some saucepans from the landlady.

"Ah, good boy," he said; "ye've got the bottles."

"They're rather dirty," Dick pointed out.

"They are? Then y'd best get a damp rag and wipe round the outsides of 'em."

"I think they need a thorough wash, inside *and* out."

"There'd be no harm, no harm at all. Ye'll find a pump in the court."

For the next two or three hours Dick worked hard, cleaning the bottles and pots as well as he could with cold water, and then writing labels in his best copperplate hand, at the doctor's direction. *O'Flynn's Cordial, O'Flynn's Sovereign Remedy, O'Flynn's Elixir*—and occasionally, to show that the doctor was open-minded and prepared to use other men's remedies, *Hill's Specific*, or *James's Powder*.

"An' put a bit of Latin underneath each one," he ordered. "Nothing like a little Latin to inspire confidence."

"What Latin must I put?"

"That's no great matter, for there's not one in ten will understand it. Ye can write what diseases it cures—or to take it three times a day, or something of that sort."

Dick considered. He had had plenty of Latin rammed down his throat at school, but he could not, for the life of him, remember many words which would do for a medicine label. *Tussis*, a cough; *morbus*, a disease; *dolor*, pain—rack his brain as he would, he could muster only the smallest medical vocabulary. Caesar's legions, as far as he could recall, had been remarkably healthy.

"Don't bother *me*," the doctor retorted when Dick

appealed to him as he stirred his pungent mixtures over the fire. "Ye *said* ye knew Latin. Very well then!"

By midday the various pots and bottles were filled and stood in rows, steaming gently, on the hearth.

"Ye can seal 'em up after dinner," said the doctor, "and stick the labels on."

"What about going to wait on the Duke, Doctor?" Dick inquired. The Irishman looked blank. "At least, you didn't say he was a duke, but I s'pose he must be if he's 'His Grace.' The one you were sent for to cure."

"To be sure, to be sure, me boy! 'Tis a good memory ye have. I shall wait upon His Grace after dinner. But in case it should slip me mind again, ye'd best fetch me from Tucker's Coffee House on the stroke of two. 'Tis only a short step along the street, towards the Strand— ye can't miss it."

Dick had his own dinner at a cheap eating house which the doctor recommended to him. At a quarter to two, having combed his hair, polished his shoes, and straightened the wrinkles in his stockings, he set off to find his master.

Coffeehouses, he was soon to learn, had their regular customers who came every day, sat in the same chairs, and treated the place as a home from home. Some were favored by authors and critics, others were full of hardheaded merchants exchanging market news. There were coffeehouses for Whigs and coffeehouses for Tories. One might be full of dandies, discussing the new fashion in waistcoats, while in another there might be Jacobites planning revolution. Tucker's, being near

Temple Bar, was a favorite haunt of the lawyers who had their chambers close by.

Dick found the great room crowded. Some gentlemen were arguing, others laughing boisterously. Here and there a lonely figure was frowning over a legal brief or idly scanning a newsletter. One had pen and ink beside him and was scribbling industriously. A vast fire blazed in the grate and a row of coffeepots stood in rank along the hearth, regular as soldiers on parade, and as brightly polished. Mrs. Tucker, a mountainous fat woman in a high-piled headdress, presided over the scene from behind a counter which, with its overhanging canopy, reminded Dick of a four-poster bed.

He saw the Irishman at one of the long tables and went over. "Excuse me, Doctor—your appointment with His Grace."

"Eh? What's that, me boy? Speak up."

Dick repeated the words more loudly, so that most of the men at the table could hear.

"Ah, the Duke, to be sure! By ye leave, gentlemen . . . I must visit me patient. Good day to ye all." The doctor reached for his hat and made a dignified exit.

Outside, a disappointment awaited Dick. His master did not require his attendance to the Duke's house. Instead, he was to go back to Mercers Court and finish the preparation of the medicines.

It was fully two hours before Dr. O'Flynn returned. He was in high good humor and, though he said nothing about his visit, it was plain that he had been received with all the courtesy due to his reputation.

The Duke must even have offered him refreshment. That much Dick could guess from his breath, which was strong enough to overcome the smell of the medicines.

Dick was kept busy during the next few weeks. Usually he accompanied his master on his visits, walking a pace behind him with his bag. And there were errands by himself to deliver medicine.

Thus he came to know London. He knew the old city of the merchants, stretching from Ludgate to the Tower. He specially loved to watch the traffic of the river—the colliers from Newcastle, the fishing boats and the grain ships, the vessels from Flanders and the Baltic, the continual scurry of the London watermen.

Sometimes he went the other way along the Strand, where fine houses lined the southern side, their front windows facing up the hill to Hampstead and their back gardens running down to the tidal mudbanks. He knew Covent Garden, with Inigo Jones's arcades designed like those of an Italian piazza, and the great square of Lincoln's Inn Fields, where gentlemen fought duels under the young plane trees.

Further west he saw the royal banqueting hall, all that remained of Whitehall Palace, since the fire in King William's time. Queen Anne now kept her state in the red-brick palace of St. James's, across the park, though she preferred to sleep in the country at Kensington and drive in daily to transact public business. The most fashionable coffeehouses were in St. James's Street, running up the hill from the palace gateway to the houses of the quality, which spread along Piccadilly and Bond Street. All this side of London was fresh, green, and countrified. Sometimes he caught, above the rumble of coach wheels and the babble of street cries, the distant shout of a huntsman or the crack of a sporting gun.

London was as fine as ever he had imagined it. It was his work which fell somewhat short of his dreams.

There were no other noblemen among the doctor's patients. The Duke himself was mentioned no more, and Dick began to suspect his very existence. The people who called upon the Irishman's skill were not exactly poor—for the poor could pay no fees—but they were small tradesmen, struggling actors and actresses, unsuccessful lawyers, and hack journalists.

"Riffraff!" snorted the Irishman, footsore from a round of such visits. "And 'tis all the patients I am like to have, so long as I live in this rathole. The world judges by appearance. Here am I, offerin' 'em me skill and learnin'—but, for lack of a new coat an' me own coach to stand at the door, I'm spurned, the way I was some ignorant quack."

"It doesn't seem fair."

" 'Tis not of meself I'm thinkin'. 'Tis all the good work I'm prevented doin', for want of the chance."

"If they only *knew* . . ."

"I've been too long away from town, me boy, that's the trouble. Two years back 'twas a different story. The tale o' me cures was on every lip."

"Isn't there any way—" Dick began doubtfully.

"Ay, me boy, there is. And ye must help me."

Dick's part in the new campaign did not appeal to him at all. When the doctor went to a coffeehouse or tavern, he had to rush in, with some pretended summons from a sickbed. Soon the doctor realized that this kind of advertisement could be gained even more easily. Dick could just as well be sent calling his name through a dozen places, even though he was at home. Once or twice, the boy was let out of the house quietly in the middle of the night, to come pelting into Mercers Court a few moments later, hammering on the door and (in a disguised voice) calling on the doctor to come at once. These midnight performances greatly increased Dr. O'Flynn's reputation.

To Dick these methods seemed no different from downright lying, and his whole nature revolted sickly against them. However, he could scarcely refuse to obey, except when the Irishman, one Sunday, wanted to be fetched out of St. Paul's in the middle of morning service. This would have been an excellent advertisement, but Dick was stubborn. The doctor was called out, nonetheless, by a ragged boy Dick had never seen before.

For the Irishman had other allies, as Dick came to learn. Men and women were paid to sit talking loudly in public places of his miraculous cures. A little spent that way, O'Flynn believed, brought a richer return than newspaper advertisements, which people were apt to disbelieve.

"Yet they'll credit anything," he sneered, "if 'tis printed in the next column—as news. An' what better news could there be, me boy, than a sick gentleman restored? I tell ye, Dick, one short paragraph, well worded, could put me on the road to fame an' fortune. The more I think of it, the surer I am."

He went off to Tucker's Coffee House with a thoughtful expression. Dick had orders to call for him at nine o'clock. When he entered Tucker's, punctual to the hour, it was obvious that something unusual was going on.

O'Flynn was on his feet, his face working with passion, his long upper lip curled back in a snarl. On the other side of the long table, calm, erect, and soldierly, stood a little man in a claret-colored coat.

"Certainly, Mr. O'Flynn, I will write something in my newspaper, to make your name better known through the town. But I doubt whether you will like what I write, for I shall keep strictly to the truth—that you are a blackguard, sir, and an impostor. In one word, a *quack!*"

A quack! The insult was like a grenade exploding in the room.

"Careful, Mr. Fazeley," squeaked one of the lawyers in horror. "That remark is actionable."

"Actionable be hanged," roared a swaggering officer in Horse Guards blue. "This isn't a matter for Lincoln's Inn, but Lincoln's Inn Fields. Won't you fight him, Paddy?"

The Irishman's color came and went. "Mr. Fazeley's suggestion is monstrous," he said between his teeth. " 'Tis beneath contempt entirely. I—I—"

All the men in the coffeehouse were on their feet. "You mean you won't challenge him, Doctor?" said the Horse Guard incredulously.

The little man in the claret-colored coat spoke again. Dick stared at him. He had a small, birdlike face, with keen blue eyes. Dick judged him to be about sixty. He must be brave, for he stood scarcely as high as the doctor's shoulder.

"Leave him alone, you old fire-eater," he told the officer in a quiet crisp voice. "I certainly have no wish to force a duel upon Mr. O'Flynn. He asked a favor of me, and I refused. He pressed me for my reasons, and I gave them."

"Ye'll apologize?" demanded the doctor.

"If you can prove me mistaken. That is quite easy." He turned to the group in general. "I shall be here to-morrow evening. If Mr. O'Flynn will bring his medical diplomas and lay them on this table, I will apologize. If not . . ." The journalist paused, with a shrug of his shoulders.

Dick looked at his master. Surely he would accept this simple challenge? Nothing could be easier than to make this Mr. Fazeley swallow his words. But O'Flynn, in that same moment, glanced sideways and saw his eager face. Something like relief shone in the green eyes.

"Ye must pardon me, gentlemen, for this once. I see my boy's come to fetch me to a case. The needs of me patients must come first. Ye'll excuse me if I don't waste me time here, answerin' the filthy accusations of a Grub Street hack." He clapped his hat on his head and marched out. Dick followed, puzzled and ashamed.

"Are you going to show them your diplomas, Doctor?" he plucked up courage to ask, the next morning.

"And why should I? A gentleman is not used to havin' his word doubted."

Dick looked unhappy. "But they *have* doubted it. And they'll doubt it still more if—"

"Let 'em! Who are they, after all? A brainless bully of a soldier—a snivelin' pack o' lawyers—and this Fazeley. Pharamus Fazeley—what a name! Did ye ever hear the like, now? And who's *he*? A third-rate scribbler, editin' a paper that's forever on its last legs! If 'twas Steele or Defoe, now, or Swift or Addison, they'd be worth powder an' shot. As 'tis, I'll not demean myself. I'll take me coffee elsewhere. Tucker's is a nasty low place, not what it was at all."

"If you'd just show them your diplomas—"

"And how *can* I show them me diplomas? Fazeley knows he's on safe ground, the cunning old snake."

"But—but you *had* diplomas? Dublin and Leyden, you said."

The doctor pulled himself up. "Of course, me boy," he said warily. "Would I be tellin' ye a lie now? But those diplomas are at the bottom o' the sea."

"At the bottom of the sea?"

"Ay, 'twas when I served as ship's surgeon. 'Twas a great battle against the French. Did I never tell ye?"

"No," said Dick, full of interest.

"Oh, 'twas a great day, with the cannons roaring an' the drums beating an' all. But just now I've a patient to see." Dr. O'Flynn fumbled in one of the big flapped pockets of his waistcoat. "There was a message from the Saracen's Head. Some sick gentleman, just arrived from Essex." He unfolded a letter and scowled at it. "Divil

take it! Here, me boy," he said passing it over, "just
give me the general drift o' this, will ye, while I pack
the bag?"

The letter was in Latin. "*Annum aetatis, post quad-
ragesimum, tertium. Temperamentum humidum, cras-
sum, catarrhis saepissime profligatum. . . .*" It was a
doctor's description of his patient's case, written in
Latin, so that it could be understood by any other medical man, at home or abroad. He began to stumble
through it, translating as best he could. O'Flynn listened with a shrewd expression. Occasionally Dick
was stumped by an unfamiliar word, but, when he appealed for help, the doctor merely grunted impatiently.
"Yes, yes, me boy, that's but a detail. 'Tis the general
drift I want."

Suddenly an imp of mischief entered Dick's head.
Looking on to the next line he saw a simple phrase ap-
proaching. *Vespere febris acerbatur,* "in the evening the
fever grows worse." Nobody who had ever learned Latin
could have forgotten a common word like *vespere.* He
frowned at the paper.

"Please, Doctor, what does *vespere* mean?"

"*Vespere?* Oh," said the Irishman carelessly, " 'tis just
a learned term—ye'd not know the word, not bein' a
doctor. Don't trouble ye head with it. I know what he
means. Go on."

But Dick did not go on. It came to him in a flash that
he had done something more than catch his master nap-
ping. He held out the letter, and said in a dry, tense
voice: "Would you translate the next bit yourself, Doctor?"

"And why should I, me boy? *Your* eyes are better than mine. What's got into ye, Dick? Why are ye lookin' at me like that?"

"I don't believe," said Dick slowly, "that you understand a word of this Latin."

The Irishman looked startled. Then he laughed. "Is it crazy ye are, me boy?"

"You said *vespere* was a learned medical term."

"An' so it is, and that's why ye didn't know it an' had to ask me. There's no English word for it at all," he added airily.

"*Vespere* is a common word. It means 'in the evening'."

The green eyes opened wider, then narrowed. He frowned at the letter. "Did ye never hear, me boy, that the Latin they talk on the Continent is quite different from the Latin they talk in England? Studyin' in Leyden, 'twas naturally the Dutchmen's Latin I learned."

It was Dick's turn to laugh. He felt himself rushing on into deeper waters than he had ever intended. "The headmaster once told us all about that," he said "He *did* say that an Englishman could hardly understand Latin when it was spoken abroad. But that's only because the foreigners pronounce it differently. It's always written the same."

There was a moment's silence between them. O'Flynn smiled. He knew when he was caught. But there was no alarm in his eyes. "Well, me boy?"

Dick licked his lips. "I don't believe you ever *were* at Leyden University," he said hoarsely. "Or at Dublin.

That man Fazeley was right. You aren't a doctor. You're just . . . what he said."

"Well?"

"It isn't honest . . . taking people's money and pretending to cure them. Why, you—you might poison them!"

"Never, me boy! There's not a drop in any of me medicines would harm a fly. An' sometimes—how d'ye know?—they might do a person a power o' good. There *have* been people have sworn I'd saved their lives."

"They'd have gotten better anyhow!"

"Who can tell? Who can ever tell?" O'Flynn's nutcracker face broke into a grin. At last Dick saw him clearly for what he was—a clever scamp with a gift for summing people up and playing on their weaknesses.

O'Flynn was all things to all men. Smooth as silk with a patient he was bamboozling into paying for a box of pills, hard as flint with Joey Rookman, the rag-and-bone man; a bold bully when he dared to be, but a slippery coward when challenged.

For a few moments Dick said nothing. The Irishman's bland charm had been wearing thin, but he had never doubted till today that he was a genuine doctor. The truth took his breath away.

"Well, my boy?" O'Flynn helped himself to snuff.

"I can't work for you any more."

"Can ye not? And you bound 'prentice to me for seven years? D'ye know what happens to 'prentices who run from their masters before their time?"

Dick knew well enough. More than once, in Abbotsbridge market place, he had heard the town crier calling the descriptions of runaway apprentices. Every newspaper contained similar announcements. Apprentices who broke their agreements were hunted like criminals. The law was all on their masters' side. But—seven years with a swindler like O'Flynn! He would rather die. For the present, however, he said nothing. He must have time to think.

The Irishman's confident mood did not last long. After dinner he burst into the room and told Dick to pack at once. "We're leavin' town for a while," he announced. "I'm goin' now to see if we can get places in the Windsor coach. Meet me at the Rising Sun, me boy, just as soon as ye can."

He was gone again, with every appearance of panic. Windsor? Dick smiled to himself thoughtfully as he got out the bags. Queen Anne was at Windsor. Before today, O'Flynn would have pretended that he was summoned to court, to advise some noble patient or even the ailing Queen herself. Such pretenses were over now between master and boy. O'Flynn could keep his lies and his play acting for other people.

He had flung down a newspaper as he left the room. Dick took it up curiously, for it was *The London Courier*, edited by Pharamus Fazeley. There were only six pages and it took him only a few seconds to find the item which had upset O'Flynn.

"We were lately approached by a certain Irish gentleman, styling himself Doctor O'F——, with the request that we should print a puff, commending his medical services to those of our readers unfortunate enough to

be sick. It is not the practice of our journal to print such puffs (though there may be others less scrupulous), but to confine our columns solely to matters of interest to the public. We think, however, that it may well be of interest to them to know that the degrees of Dublin and Leyden, claimed by the said O'F——, were in fact conferred upon him only by himself, and that . . ."

There were three paragraphs. Dick's face burned as he read them. He could not feel entirely innocent. He had not known that O'Flynn was a quack, but he had helped him in some of his tricks to win patients. What *was* he to do now?

His eye strayed to the next column. There were announcements of stolen goods, strayed animals, and—runaway apprentices. *"One John Woods, apprentice to John Snell, who ran away from his master, the boy about fifteen years of age, with a lank brown thick head of hair and a round plump pale visage; he had a light-colored coat and waistcoat, and breeches of cinnamon color."* There were girls, too, with the hue and cry after them. *"Sally Dent, about fourteen years of age, of a middle stature, with a full red face, clothed in sad-colored clothes who ran away from her master, Thomas Betts, a brick-layer."* Dick felt sorry for Sally, even though her description was not particularly attractive. He shivered. In his mind's eye he saw such an advertisement for himself: *"One Richard Arlington, about fourteen years of age, brown hair, dark eyes, of fresh coloring, clothed in a blue coat and breeches. . . ."* He sighed, stuffed the journal in his pocket, and finished packing.

O'Flynn had been wise to leave London. An angry-looking gentleman with a horsewhip was inquiring for him even as Dick slipped down the alley into Fleet Street. In every coffeehouse people would be reading that exposure in *The London Courier*. For a time, until the town forgot and went crying after some fresher scandal, there would be no patients for the Irish "doctor," but there might well be some violent visitors. There had been riots with less cause. The London mob was a terrible monster, easily roused to hunt a victim.

Windsor was crowded. Not only was the court in residence at the castle, but on the following day there was to be a new horse-race meeting at a place called Ascot, seven miles away at the far end of the Great Park.

"Then 'tis there we'll go tomorrow," O'Flynn declared, his eyes brightening. Like most Irishmen, he was fascinated by horseflesh. "We'll see the sport, me boy, and maybe we'll catch a glimpse of Her Majesty, God bless her. She's a great one for the races, I'm told, like most of her family before her."

Dick was only too pleased. It would be a holiday from O'Flynn's underhand business. Though, he felt sure, the Irishman would never get through even a day at the races without selling a box of pills to someone.

O'Flynn did not trouble him that evening. He sat drinking with a group of down-at-heel sportsmen. Only toward bedtime did he approach Dick, with an effort at that old friendly charm which had once deceived him.

"Dick, me boy, have ye any little thing of value ye could pawn?"

"Pawn? Why?" Instantly Dick was on his guard.

"Oh, 'tis a pity to go to the races and not put a little on the horse ye fancy. For meself, I'm layin' every guinea I have on Her Majesty's own horse. I'm pledgin' me watch and me snuffbox and me best suit—and 'twill all go on the one blessed animal. I tell ye, Dick, our luck's changin'. I've had some very confidential information."

"I have nothing to bet with," said Dick shortly.

"Never mind, me boy, *my* luck'll be *your* luck, just see." O'Flynn was in high spirits again. "As London didn't like us, we'll work Bath and Bristol. With money behind us we'll have fine lodgings and a carriage to stand at the door, and a fine livery for yeself, and maybe a boy to make us cups of chocolate. . . . Wait till tomorrow, only wait till tomorrow."

It was just like the Irishman. He was up or down in a moment, forever full of wild hopes or bitter self-pity. Yet tonight his confidence puzzled Dick. In his few hours at Windsor he had overheard enough talk about the race to know that the Queen's horse was not much fancied as the winner. Second place, yes—but not first. It was practically certain that the gold cup, offered by Her Majesty, would go to the Earl of Exmoor's mare, Turkish Empress. Bred from two famous strains, the Byerley Turk and the Darley Arabian, she would leave the rest of the field standing.

Yet O'Flynn was laying every penny he could raise on the next best runner!

The more Dick thought about it, the stranger it seemed. True, the odds must be very tempting. He had heard people laying twenty to one against the Queen's gelding. He could understand O'Flynn risking five guineas to win a hundred, but to risk his best suit and all his personal possessions—well, he must be an even wilder Irishman than Dick had ever realized.

Or his "confidential information" must mean that, for some secret reason, Turkish Empress had no chance of winning. . . .

"There's just one little errand," said O'Flynn. " 'Tis no further than the White Bull, in the next street. Ask for a man the name of Mitchell. He'll come out to ye— and make sure 'tis Mitchell himself, a low-built, sandy fellow, with a broken nose. I promised him this bottle of cordial."

"Mitchell, the White Bull," Dick repeated, taking the bottle, which O'Flynn fished out of his coat pocket.

Outside, he paused to glance at the bottle in the light of the lantern which swung over the doorway. It was stoppered firmly enough, but the seal was broken. For a moment he blamed his own carelessness—it was certainly one of the bottles he himself had prepared, for there was the label in his own hand. But, as he held it up, he saw that the color was much lighter than usual. Had he labeled it wrongly as well?

Better be on the safe side. He ran upstairs and got another bottle from the bag. Curiosity prompted him to take out the stopper of the first bottle and taste its contents. The results surprised him. He had learned disappointingly little of drugs while he had been in O'Flynn's service, but more, perhaps, than the Irishman had bargained for.

He was not sure exactly what was in the mixture, but

it was certainly not cordial. The smell and the bitter taste suggested liquid opium, which O'Flynn used in small quantities to deaden pain or to soothe the sleepless. Whatever it was, this mixture was powerful enough to . . . to stop a horse.

To stop a horse! Suppose that was O'Flynn's deliberate intention?

Slipping both bottles into his pockets, Dick hurried to the White Bull. A few words with a stableboy confirmed his suspicions: it was the inn where the Earl of Exmoor was staying, and also, across the yard, a no less honored guest, Turkish Empress.

Any last doubts were settled when the man Mitchell appeared. He was a shifty-looking fellow. He waddled forward with a straw between his yellow teeth, and he came from the stable yard.

"It *was* O'Flynn's Cordial you wanted?" Dick asked.

"That's the stuff, lad. In a bottle, 'e said."

"Here you are then." Dick handed him the bottle with the unbroken seal. Then he walked quickly down to the bridge and dropped the other one into the Thames. He was breathing rather fast, but it was not the result of hurried walking. He had burned his boats now. He had finished with O'Flynn.

He did not run away that night.

He needed time to think. Ever since his discovery that O'Flynn was a quack he had realized that it must come to this. Whatever the law said, he *could* not spend the next seven years of his life in bondage to a swindler.

Sooner or later he would have to cut free. But it would have been easier if he could have taken time to plan his escape and save at least a few shillings from what O'Flynn allowed him for his food.

There was no chance of that now. He must be gone before the result of the big race was known. But where? He knew only two places in the world: Abbotsbridge, which he had been so eager to leave a month or two ago, but which he now looked back upon with affection and homesickness; and London.

He had good friends in Abbotsbridge, but that was just where O'Flynn would look for him—and no friend could stand between a runaway apprentice and his lawful master. Abbotsbridge was impossible.

London then? Tossing on his bed, far into the night, he pondered the matter. He had no friends there, but it was a big place to hide in. Somehow he would find means to earn an honest living.

Next morning they joined the crowds trudging out to Ascot. O'Flynn insisted that Dick should take one bag with a supply of medicines. It was second nature with him to talk to every chance acquaintance, work every conversation around to illnesses, and finish it with the sale of some remedy. Even with the prospect of several hundred guineas glittering before his eyes, he could not break the habit.

Dick was only too pleased. It gave him the chance to bring his own small bundle hidden in the bag.

It was a brilliant summer's day. One side of the course was lined with the coaches of the nobility and gentry. There were crowds of countryfolk and Windsor tradespeople, liveried servants and red-coated soldiers, swarthy gypsies and rosy-cheeked Eton schoolboys. There were very few ladies, as usual—a race was hardly the place for them—but there was Queen Anne herself, defying convention, carrying on the sport-loving Stuart tradition, as her ancestor James the First and her uncle Charles the Second had done before her.

Dick got a close view of her as she drove onto the course—a heavy, unhealthy-looking woman of nearly fifty, plainly dressed, with dark brown hair piled high on her head in the latest fashion. She had been beautiful once, he knew, singing and dancing and acting, as a girl, in the masques and ballets at her uncle's court. Those days were gone now, and only her fine hands and her light gray eyes recalled the nymph whose part she had once played. But she looked kind, Dick thought, and she was a great queen, and he felt sorry for her, because she loved hunting and sport, but could only watch them from her carriage. He could not help wishing that her horse was good enough to win.

But it was not. O'Flynn, beside himself with excitement, had gone off to see the start, leaving Dick with the bag. This was the moment. Dick took out his own bundle and went. He was a mile away, striding eastward across country toward London, when a storm of cheering burst out behind him. He turned and listened. In a few short minutes it was over, and he went on.

Turkish Empress, he learned the next day, had won by five lengths, and had never shown better form. The Queen's horse, as expected, had come second.

4. A Dark Night in the City

London was over twenty miles away, but a country-bred
boy should manage the distance by nightfall. So he
pressed forward, through Staines and over Hounslow
Heath, stopping only to buy bread and cheese at an alehouse, and in the early evening came limping stiffly into
the city.

There had been plenty of time to think during that
walk, and he had come to a decision. He had met a
number of people during his stay in London, but all
were somehow linked with O'Flynn, and it would be
unwise to turn to any of them. He could think of only
one man who looked honest and decent, and who would
certainly not betray him to the Irishman.

For that reason he dragged himself wearily the whole length of the Strand, past Temple Bar, to Tucker's Coffee House. And there, alone in a corner, chuckling over a copy of a rival newspaper, was Pharamus Fazeley.

He glanced up, bright as a robin, when Dick spoke. "Eh? Bless my soul, aren't you O'Flynn's boy?"

"Not now, sir."

"What's the matter? Has that ruffian been beating you?"

"No, sir. I've just walked—" Dick swayed suddenly and clutched the edge of the table.

"Sit down on that bench," said the journalist crisply. He signaled to a serving-maid. Dick, leaning over the table with closed eyes, opened them quickly as the warm fumes of coffee filled his nostrils. "Drink that. The girl's bringing you a bite to eat."

Strength returned to Dick as the unfamiliar drink went down his throat. Fazeley smiled across the table. "You looked like a ghost when you came in. The ghost of Hamlet's father in the old play. *'I could a tale unfold whose lightest word . . .'*" he quoted with a chuckle.

"And I reckon I could, too," said Dick.

The journalist gave him a sharp look. "Is that why you have come to me?"

Dick stared back at him. "What do you mean, sir? I came because you looked—well, sir, you looked like somebody I could trust." He poured out the whole story of his unfortunate apprenticeship to O'Flynn.

"I see," said Fazeley. "I misjudged you. I thought that, after all, you had just come to me to . . . sell . . . O'Flynn."

"Sell O'Flynn?" Dick echoed.

"Servants *do* sell their masters, you know—especially to journalists in search of scandal. I do not like to buy my news that way, even though it may be true. I'm glad nothing of that sort was in your mind."

"It certainly was not," Dick assured him indignantly. "I thought you might help me to find work—"

"There, there, I didn't mean to ruffle you. If I can help you I will. It's the least I can do since—in a manner of speaking—it is I who have put you out of work in the first place. But—" he pulled out his watch—"it's far too late to consider such matters tonight. You are not going back to your old lodgings?"

"Oh, no, sir, but I think I can get a cheap bed—"

Fazeley silenced him with a gesture. "You don't look to me like a boy bred to the life of the gutter," he said bluntly. "If you can drag your weary limbs up Ludgate Hill you may sleep between clean sheets and save your money."

Dick's memories of that evening were muddled, but he awoke next morning to find himself in a slanty-shaped garret bedroom, with a tiny segment of St. Paul's dome framed in the window. It was the chiming of a clock which had roused him. He counted the strokes which followed. Nine! He jumped out of bed, dashed some cold water over his face at the washstand, pulled on his clothes, and opened the door cautiously.

Stairs, stairs, and more stairs went plunging down into the shadowy depths of the building. From far below came a series of heavy thuds. Of course, the explanation flashed upon him, a printing press! *The London Courier* was "printed and published by Henry Strange in Paternoster Row, by St. Paul's Cathedral." So that was where he was!

He began to go downstairs. At the first landing he caught a glimpse, through a half-open door, of Fazeley writing at a table. He looked up as Dick stood hesitating, and called him in. Sprawled at the other end of the table was a monstrously fat man in his shirt sleeves, ink-fingered and purple-cheeked, with a huge cannon ball of a head, close-cropped and uncovered by a wig.

"This is the boy, Harry. Dick, this is Mr. Strange. Have some breakfast?" Fazeley waved his hand toward an empty chair. "There's bread and butter, and—do you drink tea?"

"*Tea!*" snorted the fat man, rolling his eyes to the ceiling. "I hope the lad drinks ale with his breakfast like a Christian. How you can begin the day on a heathen Chinese pig-swill like that, Pharamus, is more than I can imagine!"

"Please," said Dick timidly, "I've never tried it, but I'd like to." Fazeley poured some of the pale amber liquid into one of the thin little porcelain bowls which served as cups.

"Poisoning yourself—at a pound a pound," said the printer gloomily. "No wonder you have the rheumatics. Your whole system must be rotted with the damp."

Dick had liked his first sip of the expensive novelty, but he now looked so concerned that Fazeley said: "Take no notice. I wish I had got my aches and pains half as pleasantly as by tea-drinking. It's an old debate between Mr. Strange and me—*he* declares I'm rotted with boiled water and dead leaves, and I say he's pickled in something stronger. Dick," he went on more seriously, "last night you babbled some tale of the race at Ascot. I want Mr. Strange to hear it."

Dick repeated the story of the Turkish Empress, the shifty stableman, and O'Flynn's Cordial. "We should print," grunted Mr. Strange. "Public interest."

Fazeley took another cup of tea. "I think you're right, Harry. Do you mind, Dick? No actual names will be given."

Dick thought for a moment. He completely agreed, this kind of thing should be exposed. "No, sir," he said hesitantly. "Only . . . O'Flynn will guess how you heard about it. It will help him to trace me—through you, sir."

"That is a point," growled Mr. Strange, rubbing his several chins. "And just now, I fancy, our Irish friend will be in a most murderous mood."

"Oh, I'm not *afraid* of him," said Dick. He had come to know the Irishman. Physical violence was not his line at all. "But I don't want him to claim me back as his apprentice."

"Is *that* all?" Fazeley looked relieved. "Was anything put into writing and signed? What we call 'indentures'?"

"Not that I saw, sir. I don't know whether the headmaster signed anything."

"But the headmaster wasn't your lawful guardian?"

"No, sir."

"Then it doesn't matter a brass farthing what he

signed on your behalf. I should be vastly surprised if anything whatever went down on paper. O'Flynn is a shy bird when it comes to the law. No, Dick—" Fazeley set down his empty cup. "You're free. He can't touch you. You can go home to Abbotsbridge, if you want to."

It was wonderful news. Yet when Dick was finally convinced, the prospect of returning to Abbotsbridge was not quite so attractive after all. Nobody likes to admit that he has been fooled. It would be no triumphant return, but a return with his tail between his legs. And the fact that Dr. Payton had also been fooled by the Irish quack would not sweeten the air.

"I would sooner stay in London, if I could find work," said Dick shyly.

The two partners exchanged glances. The journalist put his bright birdlike head on one side. The printer rubbed his chins and winked.

"I think that might be arranged, Harry?"

"I think it might, Pharamus."

So Dick joined *The London Courier*.

To Henry Strange the newspaper was only one of a dozen interests. He was a general printer, producing a constant stream of ballad sheets, almanacs, pamphlets, and books of riddles. He was equally prepared to print a volume of sermons for one of the clergy or a cheap romance of love or crime or (if possible) both. He could also be said to enjoy a full family life—all the other rooms in that tall house above the print shop, except the two occupied by Pharamus Fazeley and Dick's attic, were swarming with Stranges, large and small, male and female. Mrs. Strange was a thin, anxious, but kindly woman, usually seen as a gray shape fleeting from one floor to the next, in a despairing effort always to be in two (or better still, three) places at once.

Pharamus Fazeley was either a bachelor or a widower. His private history was never discussed in Dick's hearing. But, in one sense, he was wedded to *The Courier*.

His whole waking life was given to the collection and sifting of news for the paper. He was a familiar figure all over London, equally at home in some coffeehouse in St. James's, gathering political news, or at some tavern down-river, listening to a sea captain's report from Spain. He had contacts with a dozen foreign cities and received regular letters from his correspondents there. He himself had traveled widely. He had been with Marlborough in that great march across Europe which had ended in Blenheim. He had seen the palm-spiked islets of the Spanish Main and the green domes of Moscow. He had first met Handel, the young German whose operas were now delighting London, when they were both visiting Scarlatti in Venice. He seemed, at some time or other, to have met everyone—Purcell, Wren, Newton, Pepys, Dryden, Vanbrugh—everyone from the late King William the Third to the highwayman hanged last week at Tyburn. He was equally at home with courtiers and criminals.

"There is not," he told Dick dryly, "so much difference as you might imagine."

When not talking—or rather listening—Fazeley was usually reading or writing. All rival publications were closely studied, not merely the London papers such as *The Daily Courant, The London Gazette,* and *The Evening Post,* but (as they arrived) *The Dublin Gazette, The Edinburgh Evening Courant,* and others from the Continent, as well as the newsletters sent out by various journalists to their subscribers.

"One has to sift a deal of chaff to find a grain of truth," he explained. "Most of these papers follow one party or another, and give their news accordingly. But *The Courier* is neither Whig nor Tory. It is independent."

Possibly for that reason the paper had only a small circulation—two or three hundred copies, compared with the thousand or more sold by its rivals.

"You know, Pharamus," his partner would tell him, "people don't *want* the plain truth. They'd sooner listen to a slanging match and hear their own man saying how wicked the other fellows are. The Tories follow Swift in *The Examiner,* the Whigs follow Addison and Steele in *The Guardian.* A slanging match is what they want, and we don't give it 'em in *The Courier.*"

"What is a newspaper for?" Fazeley would retort. "To give people what they want—or the truth?"

It was always a good-humored argument, ending with dry chuckles from the editor and winks at Dick from the printer. Nonetheless, it was a worrying situation—and for nobody more so than for Dick himself. What would happen to him if *The Courier* continued to lose money and Henry Strange grew tired of paying for it from the profits of his other printing? Fazeley did not seem to have many private means of his own.

Dick's work was chiefly that of a messenger. Once more he found himself scurrying across London, searching the coffeehouses for his master, but now he could hold up his head, for he had a master who was respected in the city, and to be "Mr. Fazeley's boy" was a title of honor.

The Courier came out three times a week, though Fazeley dreamed of making it a daily. Even three issues a week took some filling, however, because he wrote almost every line himself, and he would never fill up with trivial or doubtful matter. Some of his copy was written in the copyhouses, where Dick collected it and rushed it to the printer. Fazeley was often writing and proof-correcting far into the night.

"He does too much," Strange confided to Dick. "He's not too well. He ought to go right out of London for a while, get some country air, try the waters at Bath or one of those places."

"He does look tired, Mr. Strange."

"It was the six pages that spoiled everything—both ways," said the printer darkly.

As Dick was mystified, he explained.

The government had recently brought in a Stamp Act, putting a tax on newspapers of a halfpenny or a penny per copy, according to size. At first it had looked as though this would ruin the journalists. Some publications gave up, others, such as *The Spectator*, had to double their price. Then someone had discovered a loophole in the wording of the Act: there was no mention of six-page papers. Provided a newspaper increased its size to six pages, it could avoid the tax.

"So we carry on," said Strange, "but it's made matters very difficult. It's put up our expenses—more paper, more printing. Worse than that, it's given poor Mr. Fazeley twelve columns to fill. Twelve columns, my boy! It just can't be done, you know, not with his standards of what's right and proper. There isn't so much news in the world, not three times a week."

As the weeks passed Dick could see that the fat, kindly printer was growing more and more worried about his partner's health. At last, in August, when the court was out of London, Parliament not sitting, and the circulation of *The Courier* at its lowest, he took a firm line. "Suspend publication," he urged. "Take a rest for a month or two, and then see."

"Let *The Courier* die?" said Fazeley sadly.

"We can start it again in the autumn, maybe, or even something better. Look at Addison and Steele! They ran *The Tatler*—then they started *The Spectator* —now it's *The Guardian*. It's no shame to have a few ups and downs, so long as you come up fighting next time."

Fazeley considered for a few moments. "Very well," he sighed. "Shall we just continue to the end of this week?"

Dick listened in silence. What was he to do now? The answer came on a black, stormy wet night two days later. And it came to him, most mysteriously, in a sedan chair.

"That man interests me greatly," murmured Fazeley, setting down his empty coffee cup.

It had been an evening of livid skies and thunder growling round the city. Night had come early. The candles were lit in Wilkins's Coffee House, close by the Royal Exchange, and, though it was still August, the big coal fire was more than welcome.

Dick was sitting with Fazeley on a high-backed settle at one side of the room. He followed his master's glance. A heavily built, prosperous-looking old man was enthroned in an armchair on the far side of the fireplace. His lips were pursed thoughtfully, his hands clasped over the end of his stick, and his florid face tilted toward his younger companion, who was expounding something in an eager undertone.

"Yes, sir," Dick agreed in a whisper. "He looks very important. Is he the Lord Mayor?"

The journalist smiled. "Who? The old man? Oh, no. But he's a goldsmith and banker, one of the richest men in the city. It is the other one who stirs my curiosity."

Dick looked again. The second man wore a plain riding coat years out of fashion and his own black hair, long, instead of a wig—a thing which might still do well enough in a remote part of the country but was hardly suitable for town. His voice had a North Country ring.

"Now why," murmured Fazeley, "is our wealthy banker listening so patiently—you might almost say, so respectfully—to a rough-tongued, shabby-looking fellow like that? Have another look at him, Dick, when he turns his head."

Dick obeyed. He saw then that the man had a striking face. He was perhaps forty, not handsome, and without any fineness of feature such as went with gentle breeding. It was a face of strength and power, though; gaunt as a weather-beaten crag. The eyes burned with restless energy, the lines of the mouth showed a dogged, relentless purpose.

"He looks like a strong sort of character," he murmured.

"I would rather have him as a friend than as an enemy," commented Fazeley with a laugh. "And as an editor with an issue of *The Courier* still to get out, I should greatly like to know what he is saying."

"Have you any idea who he is, sir?"

"Oh, yes. His name is Charles Mount. He comes from Derbyshire. He is a silk manufacturer, in a small way."

"Silk?"

"Yes. That may be why the banker is listening so hard. There's money in silk." He considered for a moment. "Mount turned up in London a few days ago, to raise a loan for some scheme he has in mind. What it is, I have no notion. I *think* he is honest. He looks it. But I am anxious to know more."

"And put it in *The Courier?*"

"If that seemed in the public interest. If it were not such gross bad manners to interrupt the gentlemen, I should dearly love to step across the room and scrape acquaintance. Perhaps, if we sit here a little longer, there may be an opportunity."

In this, though, the journalist was unlucky. At that moment a group of merchants called him over to ask his advice on a point concerning the East India Company. While he was thus engaged, the two men rose suddenly to their feet, and made their farewells in normal tones.

"My coach is at the door, Mr. Mount. It's a dirty night. Would you care to—"

"Thank ye, no, Alderman. I'm staying in Salisbury Square, quite the other direction—at Mr. Cogwell's. I'll take one of them sedan chairs."

"As you please, sir. Good night, then."

The banker limped goutily through the door. Mr. Mount stood for a few moments by the fire, helping himself to snuff, while a waiting-girl poked her head out into the rain and called shrilly to the chairmen sheltering somewhere outside. Dick took the opportunity to study him over the top of a newspaper—until he realized that he himself, like everyone else in the room, was being studied by Mr. Mount. Fazeley and the merchants clustered round him . . . the two thin brothers arguing in ill-tempered undertones . . . the fat little man dozing in a corner, his feet comically spread out and the clay pipe dangling from his fingers . . . the sallow foreign gentleman writing at the table. . . . The shrewd gaze of the North Country man flickered over every figure in turn. There was a wariness in those eyes—something more (Dick fancied) than just the natural canniness of a trustful businessman.

It was as though Mr. Mount were looking for something, or rather somebody, yet not very much wanting to find him. Once his eyes narrowed and he frowned, and his head went down a little, with the movement of a bull mindful to charge.

All this took only a few moments. The door opened again and two chairmen shambled into the candlelight, their coats darkly spotted with rain.

"Where to, sir?" inquired the leading chairman. He let go the carrying poles, slipped the leather slings from his shoulders, and stood aside, opening the door of the sedan with a bow.

"Salisbury Square—Mr. Cogwell's," said Mr. Mount tersely. He stepped between the shafts and, with a smart click of the door, had boxed himself in before the chairman could stir a finger.

"Salisbury Square it is, sir. Come on, Sam." The men picked up the chair again, and went out into the dripping blackness.

"I'm afraid you've missed your chance, sir," said Dick when Fazeley returned. The whole coffeehouse was beginning to empty now. Only the sleeping fat man showed no sign of departure.

"A pity." Fazeley clucked with vexation. "I should have liked—" He broke off and strode quickly across to where Mount and the alderman had been sitting. "One of them left a snuffbox," he said, his hand darting down between the two empty coffee cups. "Not the alderman, I think—it is too plain."

"It was the other man's," said Dick. "Mr. Mount's. I saw it in his hand. Shall I run after him? I heard him say where he was staying. I could catch him before he's halfway there."

"Don't," said Fazeley, with a smile. "Give him another five minutes' start. I am particularly anxious to make his acquaintance. This snuffbox will serve as an introduction—but the opportunity will be wasted if you overtake him in the street."

Few people were about at that late hour. Here and there the wet darkness was broken by an overhanging lantern or the light streaming from a window, or the fiery blob of a linkboy's torch. Otherwise the night was one of unrelieved blackness, with not a star to pierce the curtain of the clouds. Even the vast bulk of St. Paul's was invisible.

Fortunately Dick now knew the highways and byways of the city. Salisbury Square was just off Fleet Street, near his original lodgings with O'Flynn. He had to go down the steep hill below the cathedral, through Ludgate, and over the bridge spanning the Fleet River. He doubled his caution here, remembering that some repairs were being done and having no wish to trip over a block of stone or bury his nose in a pile of earth. The rain was hissing down, and he could hear the Fleet swirling angrily along its channel to join the Thames.

Not for the first time he wished that people would agree to number their houses, but it was too much to hope that Englishmen would ever combine to do anything so sensible. At last, after inquiry at two other houses, he found Mr. Cogwell's. His knock was answered by an elderly footman.

"Please," said Dick, "is this where Mr. Mount is staying?"

"It is, my lad. But he's not in yet."

It was Dick's turn to look surprised. "Oh! Then he must have gone a longer way round." He himself had, he remembered, taken some short cuts through alleys a sedan might avoid.

"Mr. Mount is expected at any moment," said the footman. He looked anxious to get to bed.

"Well, he can't be long. He left Wilkins's Coffee House in front of me, and I heard him give the chairmen this address."

"Have you a message for him?"

"Yes. From Mr. Fazeley. Of *The London Courier*."

"Then you'd better step inside and wait."

Dick obeyed thankfully. His hat was dripping, his shoulders dark with wet, his stockings and shoes streaked with mud. The square, paneled hall, with its candlelight, was a welcome refuge from the drizzle.

"Mr. Mount left his snuffbox," he explained. "I've brought it with Mr. Fazeley's compliments, and he'll do himself the honor to call on Mr. Mount in the morning."

"H'm." The old footman sniffed doubtfully. "I don't know as Mr. Mount wishes to meet journalists. But it was civil to send you through all this rain. Ah," he said, as the professional rat-tat of a chairman was heard, "this sounds more like our gentleman."

He opened the door again, peered out, then flung it wide. The two chairmen walked carefully across the threshold and set down the sedan. They, and it, were extremely wet—the glass windows of the chair were so mottled with raindrops that the occupant was invisible. The man in front stepped from between the shafts, swept off his hat with a bow, and laid his other hand on the door handle of the sedan.

"Here ye are, sir," he announced. "Mr. Cogwell's house, safe, sound, and as dry as a bone." Then, as he swung back the door, he gave a gasp of amazement.

There was no passenger on the seat inside.

Instantly there was consternation in the hall. The other chairman dived round to see what was the matter. Dick and the footman sprang forward. Everyone exclaimed at once. The raised voices brought Mr. Cogwell hurrying down the staircase. The merchant was an elderly man, slippered and bespectacled, with an open book clutched in his hand.

"Thomas! What's happening?"

The footman began to explain. The chairmen interrupted to defend themselves. Dick chimed in to support the first part of their story. He recognized them. He had seen Mr. Mount step into their sedan and heard him give this address.

"But—but it's impossible!" wailed the old merchant distractedly. "A man can't *vanish* from a chair like that." He stared fiercely at the two frightened chairmen. "I know you fellows well by sight. Otherwise I'd suspect some villainy."

"We been carrying chairs in the city this twenty year, Mr. Cogwell," said the first man, squaring his shoulders, "an' never a word breathed against our characters."

"I know, I know. But . . . did you come straight here from Wilkins's Coffee House?"

"Straight here, sir. Keeping to the main streets, sir."

"Is your chair bewitched then? You mean to tell me that Mr. Mount simply disappeared during the journey —into thin air? Mr. Mount is a fair-sized gentleman. Can't you tell any difference when you have someone in the chair and when you haven't?"

The two men turned and gaped at each other.

"I never felt no difference, did you, Sam?"

"No, Matt, I can't say as I did."

Dick stooped forward in front of the sedan. He broke in upon their talk. "No wonder they didn't, sir. Look here."

"What's that? Thomas, hold the candle so I can see!"

Three heavy slabs of masonry were revealed. One lay on the seat, half covered by a cushion. The other two were on the floor of the sedan.

"Well, I'll be hanged!" gasped the first chairman. "Now we know why it was still heavy—"

"Yes, you fool," said the old merchant sharply, "but we still don't know how Mr. Mount changed into three pieces of stone. You'd better be careful, my good man. You may have to answer for this before the magistrates."

"I vow to you, Mr. Cogwell, sir—"

"Listen. Are you positive you came straight here without making a call or stop of any kind?"

"Positive, sir. Sam here will bear me out."

"Just a moment, Matt," said his partner. "True enough, we didn't call anywhere, but we did stop, ye remember."

"Ah, that's right, so we did. It was just by the Fleet Bridge, Mr. Cogwell. The gentleman tapped on the glass, so of course we stopped. He reckoned he'd heard a shout, an' thought someone had fallen in the river."

"Go on."

"Well, sir, we'd heard nothing, and it didn't seem hardly likely, but he would have us take my lantern and look about. O' course, we couldn't see anyone—the night was pitch black—an' after a minute he calls us back.

'Don't waste any more time,' he yells, sharp-like. An' we hears him slam the door again—which of course he'd opened to speak to us—so we went back, picked up the chair, and came straight on here."

"That's gospel truth, sir," agreed Sam.

The merchant considered for a moment. "Are you sure it was Mr. Mount's voice, that second time?"

The chairmen rubbed their chins and scratched their heads. There was something comic in the way the two workmates, from long partnership, had grown alike in look and gesture.

"Wouldn't swear to it," said Matt.

"You see, Mr. Cogwell," Sam supported him, "we'd only heard the gentleman speak a few words before. He was sort of sharp. And he never spoke to us again. It's hard to be sure, really."

"Then," said Mr. Cogwell grimly, "he may have been kidnaped in those few moments when you left the chair. Murdered even—"

"*Murdered?*"

A girl's voice, young and clear, echoed the word. They all turned their heads to the broad staircase. The girl was halfway down. One hand gripped the heavy oak balustrade, the other held a candlestick. She was in a loose dressing gown, ready for bed, and her hair, red as a fox, was loose on her shoulders. Dick guessed she was about thirteen.

"Has—has something happened to Uncle?"

The old merchant met her as she reached the foot of the stairs and put an arm around her shoulder.

"Don't distress yourself, Celia. We are rather anxious

about Mr. Mount, but we know nothing for certain."
He told her what the chairmen said. Her eyes opened
wider.

"But who would do a thing like that to Uncle Charles?
I don't understand."

"Nor do I," said Mr. Cogwell heavily. "But London's
a lawless city nowadays. There's some mystery here, but
who's to solve it I don't know. We shall have to think.
The watch are precious little use. If your uncle does not
come home, we can go to a magistrate first thing in the
morning."

"May I say something, sir?" put in Dick. The girl
swung round, noticing him for the first time.

"Yes, yes, boy," said the merchant. "What is it?"

"My master could help you, if anyone could. He
knows the underworld of London, sir—they say no honest man knows it so well."

"Indeed. And who is your master?"

"Pharamus Fazeley, sir, of *The London Courier*—"

"Fazeley! By all means. Celia, my dear," said Mr.
Cogwell in a brighter tone, "if there is one man in London who can solve this puzzle, it is Pharamus Fazeley!"

5. A Summons for Celia

"May I fetch Mr. Fazeley now?" asked Dick eagerly.

"We should be vastly obliged," said Mr. Cogwell. "Mr. Mount is not one to play foolish jokes. Yet I should like someone else's advice before going to the Justices."

"I'll be off then, sir."

"Take care of yourself," the girl called with a little shiver. Dick laughed reassuringly as he ran through the door, but he could have done with his father's pistol for company. The night, which had been merely black and wet before, was now full of menace. Something unusual, something perilous, was stirring in the city. If Charles Mount—who looked strong as a bullock—had been plucked from inside his sedan, what might not happen to a solitary boy? When he neared the bridge where the sedan had halted and the stones must have been substituted for the passenger, he looked right, left, and behind him, straining his ears for the slightest movement. Then, heedless of potholes and puddles and repair materials, he lowered his head and pelted across. He did not slacken his pace until he reached the printing house in Paternoster Row.

Fazeley was writing in his sitting room upstairs. He snuffed the air like a war horse when Dick blurted out what had happened. He was on his feet in a moment. "Tell me the details as we go. Mr. Charles Mount becomes more and more interesting. I think . . . yes, I think—just to be on the safe side." He opened a drawer and took out a pistol, loaded it with the speed bred of experience, and slipped it into his pocket. "I doubt if *we* shall run into any adventures," he said with a regretful chuckle, "but one never knows."

"Would your bullets fit *my* pistol?" Dick asked.

"Not tonight." Fazeley chuckled again and patted his shoulder. "I promise I'll teach you how to handle that weapon of yours—but not tonight. I've no fancy to have a beginner blazing away behind me in the darkness."

They reached Salisbury Square without incident. In the meantime the two chairmen had been refreshed with tankards of ale, but they remembered no further details likely to help in solving the mystery. Fazeley knew both men well as honest characters, so, after their addresses had been noted, they were allowed to go.

Mr. Cogwell led the way upstairs to the drawing

room, where the fire had been made up and a decanter of wine set out, with glasses, to assist the gentlemen in their conference.

The girl, Celia, had taken advantage of the interval to dress and do her hair. She was smart, Dick realized, as well as good-looking—not at all the kind of niece he would have expected the homely Mr. Mount to possess. Whereas his coat had been cut in the fashion of the last reign, the girl wore one of the new hooped skirts in a creamy brocade, spangled with tiny green flowers.

"I wished Miss Mount to join us," said the old merchant. "Young though she is, she is Mr. Mount's only near relative—"

"And he is mine," cut in the girl. She sat straight in her chair, very self-possessed. Was she very brave, Dick wondered, or just hard?

Her calm was partly explained when Fazeley offered her his sympathy. She must be very distressed. . . .

"I *am*, Mr. Fazeley. Uncle Charles has been so kind to me. And I know I am going to get extremely fond of him."

"*Going?*" Fazeley echoed, his eyebrows rising. It was seldom the little journalist revealed his surprise so obviously.

"I never saw him until two weeks ago."

"Miss Mount was brought up in America, in Virginia," Mr. Cogwell explained hurriedly. "It is very sad—"

"My parents were drowned," she said in a low, controlled voice. "As I had no other relatives there was nothing to do but come to Uncle Charles. He has been most generous." Her fingers caressed the rich brocade of her skirt. "But naturally we do not know each other very well yet. Mr. Cogwell has been asking me if Uncle had any enemies. I have no idea."

"I fear that I cannot be much more helpful," said the old merchant. "I have dealt with Mr. Mount for some years past. But only in the way of business, you know. I think he only accepted my invitation to stay here because of the young lady."

"We came straight here from Bristol," said the girl. "Uncle met me when I landed. I am to live with him in Derbyshire, but I have not been there yet. Now, of course . . ." She broke off. This time there was a slight shakiness in her voice.

"Tell me," said Fazeley quickly, twiddling the stem of his empty glass, "has your uncle shown any sign of nervousness since he arrived in London? Has he received any sort of threat—any demand for money?"

"If he had, I don't think he would have told me. Uncle Charles is very . . . well, he does not talk much."

"I understand. Even so, you might have noticed something?"

Celia Mount wriggled her narrow shoulders. "My uncle often seems strange," she answered reluctantly. "Perhaps that is my fault." She gave an apologetic little laugh. "I am always being told I talk too much. Uncle Charles is not married and isn't used to young people. I expect he thinks I am very silly."

"He lives for his business," interrupted Mr. Cogwell. He sounded approving. Business was what a man ought to live for. Young girls with red hair and billowing brocade hoop skirts were all very pretty, but the real world was the mill and the countinghouse. He turned to Fazeley. "Surely, if poor Mr. Mount *has* met with foul play, might he not have had any warning beforehand? Gentlemen are frequently set upon in the dark streets and robbed. You know yourself, sir—"

"I know a good deal about the criminal classes of the town," interrupted Fazeley, "and about their methods. I know those who snatch and run, those who use clubs, those who hold you up at the pistol point. But I have yet to hear of any who specialized in spiriting their victims out of sedan chairs, and substituting stones of roughly the same weight!"

"It is certainly remarkable," agreed Mr. Cogwell.

"Note how the spot was selected: the Fleet Bridge was the one place where loose building materials were lying handy. Then the mysterious cry Mr. Mount thought he heard. The most mysterious feature of *that* is that neither of those worthy fellows admits to hearing a cry at all."

At that moment the door opened and the old footman shuffled in with every appearance of excitement and relief.

"It's all right, sir! The gentleman's quite safe, sir!"

"Is my uncle back?" cried the girl, starting up.

"No, miss, he won't be back tonight. But he's sent a message, sir."

"For me? Where is it?" Mr. Cogwell replaced his spectacles on his nose.

"Oh, it's not a note, sir. Just word of mouth. Mr. Mount's compliments, sir, and his apologies. Unexpected business. He'll write and explain everything later."

"*Write?*" exclaimed the merchant. "Isn't he coming back? Who brought this message?"

"Just a boy, sir. Might have been a boy from an inn."

"Where is he?" broke in Fazeley sharply. "Can we have him in here, Mr. Cogwell?"

"Beg your pardon, sir," said the footman unhappily, "but he didn't wait."

"Didn't wait!" Mr. Cogwell exploded. "Thomas, you're a slubbering blockhead. 'Pon my word—"

"Have you given us the whole message?" Again it was Fazeley's crisp, quiet voice.

"No, sir. He'll explain when he writes, sir, but just now he's compelled to leave town at short notice."

"What about me?" the girl demanded.

"Mr. Mount says you're to pack your things and his. And will the master be good enough to put you in a hackney coach tomorrow morning, and tell the man to drive you to Hampstead Heath. Mr. Mount will be looking out for you on the road there at eight o'clock, just beyond the last of the houses."

"What inn did this boy come from?" asked the merchant.

"He wouldn't say, sir. I did ask. But . . ."

"Then we have no means of checking if this message is genuine," said Fazeley. He turned to the girl. "Does this message *sound* like your uncle?"

"Oh, yes. Very blunt. Not a word wasted. Do this, do that, be in such a place at such a time. It could very easily come from Uncle Charles."

"But does it?" grumbled Mr. Cogwell. "My dear young lady, I don't think I could possibly send you off to Hampstead like this—"

"But you must, Mr. Cogwell! Uncle Charles would be furious if I weren't there."

"You want to keep this appointment?" asked Fazeley.

"I daren't *not* keep it."

The journalist looked at Mr. Cogwell. "I think she had better, you know. It is our only link with Mr. Mount—or the people who have spirited him away."

"But, Mr. Fazeley, what if it is a trap—another kidnaping? Even in daylight, the Heath is a dangerous place. Suppose she gets to Hampstead, and it is not her uncle who is waiting for her?"

Mr. Fazeley smiled. His tired face was suddenly younger, as though the excitement and mystery were acting as a tonic.

"Young Dick, here, and I will be there to lend a hand."

It was a short night's sleep for Dick. No sooner had he dropped off, it seemed, than Fazeley was beside him, gently shaking his shoulder. It was scarcely dawn. A pale pewter-gray light gleamed softly through the attic.

"Coffee," said Fazeley. "Nothing like it at this hour. Get your clothes on and come down."

Five minutes later Dick joined him at the table. The far end was littered with closly written sheets of paper. Henry Strange was sprawled in his usual chair, a tankard at his elbow.

"There's the last issue of *The Courier*," Fazeley was

saying, with a wave of the hand toward the papers. "I sat up most of the night." Dick stared at him. Fazeley looked as dapper as usual.

"Thanks," said the fat man gloomily. "So all I'll have to do is to correct the proof sheets for you—and slip in a paragraph about the late Mr. Pharamus Fazeley?"

"On the contrary," chuckled the editor. "I may be pestering you this afternoon to take out two columns and set fresh type for the remarkable story of the vanishing silk manufacturer and the romantic affair of Hampstead Heath." He stood up, wiping his lips. "Give me that pistol of yours, Dick, and I'll show you how to load it. If you're old enough to come on this little excursion, I suppose you are old enough to be trusted with firearms."

Dick passed it over, listening carefully to Fazeley's instructions.

"Hold it like this, Dick—your second finger on the trigger and your forefinger lying along the barrel."

"I should have thought the forefinger would have been the obvious one for pulling the trigger?"

"The obvious, maybe, but not the best. You see, if you ever have to shoot at a man—and heaven forbid you'll need to this morning!—you need to be quick, or he'll shoot you first. That means you have no time to aim, probably. It's up with your pistol—bang!—and hope for the best. If your forefinger lies along the barrel, it's only the same action as pointing quickly at something, and you've made that movement so often in ordinary life that you shouldn't be far off the mark."

"What a good idea! Of course, where my finger points, the pistol points too."

"Practically, yes. And, by the way, don't talk of 'pulling' the trigger. However hurried you are, try to make it more of a squeeze. If you pull, your shots go all over the place."

"I always understood that Hampstead Heath was full of dangers," said the printer, rolling his eyes to the ceiling. "I wouldn't go near it today for a thousand guineas."

"Don't mind Mr. Strange," said Fazeley with a twinkle in his own eye. "He's just disappointed that he can't join us. But Mrs. Strange won't let him."

"A man must consider his wife and children," the printer lamented. "But there it is, good luck to both of you. And, Pharamus, take care of the boy."

"I will," Fazeley promised cheerfully.

A hackney coach was already standing outside Mr. Cogwell's house when they got there, and the footman was helping to lift various boxes down the front steps and to strap them in position over the back wheels. The old merchant was fussing about in the hall, maids were running up and down stairs on last-minute errands, and Miss Celia Mount, mantled and hooded against the early morning air, seemed by far the calmest member of the household.

"I hope we are doing right," Mr. Cogwell kept muttering. "I don't like it. I don't feel happy at all."

"But why not?" The girl's gray-green eyes were dancing with amusement. "I feel sure Uncle Charles sent that message. And—even if he didn't—what harm can I come to, with these gentlemen to take care of me?"

"Don't worry about her," Fazeley urged him. "We won't leave her until we see her safely in her uncle's keeping. And, when we get back, Dick shall bring you word that all is well."

They took their seats, and the coach rumbled away.

"Mr. Cogwell is a kind old man," said Miss Mount decidedly, "but he fusses. One might think I was a child."

"Hampstead *is* a wild place," Fazeley pointed out gently. "If Mr. Mount were better acquainted with these parts he might have hesitated before naming it as a meeting place."

"Uncle Charles never stops to think of such things. Wild!" she echoed. "You forget I come from America. That is wild, if you like. There were Indians quite near to us there. Even we girls learned to shoot. One never knew." Dick would have dearly loved to question her about the Indians, but she swept on before he could speak. "Everyone in London exclaims when they hear I am going to live in Derbyshire. So *wild*, they say! Because there are some rocks and caves, and the post takes several days from London. Is it no wilder than that, Mr. Fazeley?"

"I have never been there, Miss Mount—"

"You must call me Celia, please. I am not *so* old. People in London are much too polite and stiff, I think."

"Thank you, Celia." Fazeley smiled. "I wish my newspaper were continuing. Your impressions of London would have given me good material. No, I have never seen the wonders of Derbyshire, though I should enjoy doing so."

"What wonders are there?"

"Oh, sparkling caverns, rivers that vanish, mountains that shiver, bottomless pits—"

"Uncle Charles hasn't told me about any of these! He only says they make good cloth there."

"Every man to his own interest. I confess myself that, as I get older, these marvels appeal to me less. I think I would rather have a few days fishing in those trout-filled rivers Izaak Walton wrote about."

"How dull!" The girl made a face. "Don't you think so, Dick?"

"The caverns sound more interesting, Miss Celia."

"Don't call me miss!" she ordered. "You're not a servant, are you?"

Dick was embarrassed. Fazeley came to his rescue. "Certainly not," he said warmly. "Dick has been my assistant on *The London Courier*. What he will do now —what I shall do myself—now that the last issue for the time being has gone to press . . . well, that is still quite unsettled."

The coach rumbled on over the cobbles. Gradually the densely packed city gave place to leafy suburbs. A damp, silvery mist hung over everything, and the houses loomed as dim gray shapes. Just the kind of morning, Dick thought, for highwaymen to be busy! It was good to feel the pistol heavy against his thigh.

Celia displayed no uneasiness. She chatted briskly all

the time, asking questions about *The Courier* and what Dick had done before. He found himself pouring out his whole life story.

"And you don't know what you will do now? I shall tell Uncle Charles about you. Would you like to come up to Derbyshire and make silk?"

"It's—it's very kind of you, Celia." The girl's direct methods left him rather breathless. "I'll have to wait and see what happens."

"You do," she said graciously. "But I know Uncle said he was always on the lookout for what he calls 'a likely lad.' I don't know what that means, but I'm sure you're likely if anyone is."

"Thank you," Dick muttered, choking quietly in his corner.

It was now nearly eight o'clock and the steep slope of Hampstead rose in front. Celia began to show the first signs of nervousness. But it was not due to any fear that the message had been a false one: it was doubt as to what her uncle would say when she arrived with an escort of strangers.

Fazeley guessed the trouble. The horses were having great difficulty as the hill grew steeper, and he seized on this as a convenient excuse. "I think it would be better if Dick and I got out and walked," he said. "We might as well say our goodbys now. We shall keep close behind the coach until we see you safely into Mr. Mount's care."

"Do you mind?" she said anxiously. "Uncle Charles is so strange. He cannot bear what he calls 'people interfering,' even when they are being kind."

So their farewells were quickly said, and her two pro-
tectors got out, telling the coachman to drive on.

"I thought you were so anxious to meet Mr. Mount?"
said Dick with a puzzled look.

"So I was," admitted Fazeley ruefully. "I am utterly
perplexed by last night's doings. But, even if it *is*
Charles Mount waiting for Celia on the Heath, he does
not look the sort of man to pour out explanations to
strangers at the roadside. And if it is *not* he who sent
the message, but somebody else . . ." The little journalist paused significantly.

"What if it isn't?" Dick prompted him.

"Then I would sooner meet him—or them—on equal
terms, out in the open," said Fazeley grimly, "than
cooped up in that coach with the girl!"

They were now on the summit of the hill. They had
to quicken their steps to keep the coach in view, a dim
gray shape lurching from side to side. The last houses
fell behind them. The road ran across the open heath,
which was dotted with trees and furze bushes.

"He's slowing down," said Fazeley suddenly.

"Yes. Look, sir, there's another carriage drawn up
ahead. I can see *two* men. Oh, I think one's only the postilion."

"We'll make sure."

He led the way forward, using the cover of the furze
bushes. Dick kept obediently at his side, admiring the
coolness with which Fazeley bore himself at a moment
like this. His own blood was racing. At all costs, he told
himself, he must keep calm and do nothing foolish. The
pistol was safe enough till it was cocked.

The hackney coach came to a standstill. The other vehicle, they could now see, was a post chaise. One of the figures wore a peaked riding cap and boots. He was, as Dick had guessed, the postilion. The other man was familiar. It was the silk manufacturer, still in the same shabby coat, just as they had seen him in Wilkins's Coffee House the evening before. If they had had the slightest doubt, it was removed when cheerful voices rang through the morning air.

"Good morning, Uncle Charles!"

"Ah, good lass! I thought it were you!"

Fazeley and Dick stood behind the screen of furze bushes while the boxes were transferred to the back and roof of the chaise. They saw the girl turn, while her uncle was settling with the coachman, and blow them a kiss.

"So that's that," said Dick, feeling a little flat as the door of the chaise slammed, the postilion climbed into the saddle of the left-hand horse, and the Mounts drove happily away.

It seemed a feeble and unsatisfactory ending to the affair.

"I'm afraid so," began Fazeley with a regretful shrug. Then suddenly his tone changed. "I am not so sure," he whispered, and flung out an arm to point.

Three figures were flitting through the bushes on the opposite side of the road. They seemed to be in a great hurry, yet anxious not to be seen. It was as though they had been trying to overtake the coach, before, and were now transferring their attention to the chaise. Certainly the coach seemed to be of no further interest to them, for, as it came slowly rumbling back, they made no attempt to stop it.

"Come on, Dick," said Fazeley, starting after them as they vanished into the mist ahead. "I think we shall have to run!"

6. A Shadow Singing

"Help!"

A pistol cracked.

"Help!" came Celia's voice again. "Uncle, look—" Her last cry was suddenly muffled.

As Dick came out of the mist he grasped the situation in one swift glance.

The chaise was slued across the road. The postilion was spread-eagled in the mud, motionless. Celia was struggling in the arms of a man, her head enveloped in a cloak. Her uncle had jumped out, and was battling frenziedly with the other two strangers. He still gripped a pistol, but he was unable to reload it, for his arms were held. All three attackers wore black masks.

Dick cocked his own pistol as he ran forward, letting out a loud yell to announce his approach. It had the desired effect. The first stranger let Celia go. She sprawled sideways and nearly pitched out of the carriage.

"Hands up!" panted Dick. The man leaped down, a long knife flashing like a streak of light. Dick leveled his pistol. There was no time, in the flurry, to remember Fazeley's instructions. The pistol went off with a flash and a bang, but the bullet whined harmlessly over the bushes, and the man came on with upraised knife.

Crack!

This time it was Fazeley's pistol. The masked man howled as blood splashed from his arm. He stopped short, and, after a moment's hesitation, dashed away into the undergrowth. Seeing themselves outnumbered, his companions followed.

"Shall we go after them?" gasped Dick.

Fazeley shook his head, too breathless to answer. Mr. Mount was reloading. Celia had picked herself up and came forward.

"You all right, lass?"

"Yes, Uncle; are you?"

"Ay. Thanks to these gentlemen. Why," he added, staring at Dick, "you're naught but a lad."

Fazeley was kneeling over the postilion.

"He's coming round," he said, producing a small flask and setting it to the man's lips. "I think it's just a knock on the head."

"Ay, that was it," Mr. Mount confirmed. "They tumbled him out of his saddle and knocked him down. I was out in a flash, myself, but they were on me before I could take proper aim. I'm uncommonly obliged to you, sir, and the lad here." His stern features broke into a smile of rare warmth.

The postilion sat up, asking after his horses and declared that he would be all right in a minute. Fazeley rose, brushing his knees, and shook the manufacturer's hand.

"No, it is not just a fortunate accident that we came along," he explained frankly. "We were at Mr. Cogwell's last night when your message arrived. Mr. Cogwell was a little worried in case the message should not have come from you—"

"Not come from me?" echoed Mr. Mount.

"Well, it wasn't written, you know, Uncle," Celia pointed out. "And you never sent any sort of token to prove it was from you."

"Why the heck should I?" Mr. Mount scratched his head. "Something very unexpected turned up. . . . I slept at the Bell Savage Inn, as it happened. It were so late, I'd no time to trouble wi' pen and paper. It never crossed my mind you'd start fancyin' things—"

"It was natural enough—" began Celia, but her uncle's smile had faded. Fazeley said quickly:

"I think, sir, it would be better not to stay here. If you will let us, we'll keep you company across the Heath."

"Nay, there's no need—"

"Oh, please, Uncle!" Celia begged. "It was all so frightening. And the poor postilion must be feeling very shaken still."

It was a tight fit, but they managed to pack into the

chaise; the postilion climbed stiffly into the saddle, and off they went.

There was little conversation for the next few minutes. Everyone preferred to keep a wary eye for any further attack. But soon the sun broke through, and houses appeared in front.

"Have you any idea who those fellows were?" inquired Fazeley.

Mr. Mount seemed both surprised and vexed by the question. "No idea at all! These highwaymen are all round London, aren't they, like wasps around a honeypot?"

"They were not the usual highwaymen type," mused Fazeley. "They had masks, true—but no horses. And no pistols."

"One came at me with a knife," said Dick proudly.

"That in itself was unusual. Unless they were foreigners. And another thing: *what did they want?*"

"What do highwaymen usually want?" retorted Mr. Mount. "Ordinary common thieves, that's what they were."

"Well, sir," said Fazeley mildly, leaning across to offer him a pinch of snuff, "they were your highwaymen, not mine. Far be it from me to interfere with another gentleman's property!" He turned the conversation deftly to other matters, but Dick felt that the journalist's curiosity was no more satisfied than his own.

The talk was now all of fishing, the only relaxation Mr. Mount permitted himself from the cares of business. Dick himself had no interest in the sport, so he gave himself up to his own thoughts.

There was plenty to think about.

Mr. Mount was unwilling to discuss the highwaymen. Did he know more about them than he would admit, and, if so, why was he concealing his knowledge? Where had he been last night? What was the truth about his disappearance from the sedan chair?

Link by link Dick hammered out a chain of reasonable explanations.

Mr. Mount had received some kind of warning last night. The danger, whatever it was, was so compelling that he had decided to leave London at once.

To throw his enemies off the scent he had stopped the chairmen by the Fleet Bridge, where he had previously noticed heaps of building materials, and had placed the stones inside the sedan. Then he had called impatiently to the men, slammed the door—but from the outside— and stepped back into the inky darkness until they had trudged out of hearing.

Only with a sedan was such a trick possible, for on a wet night it would be carried right into the house at the other end of the journey, and a shadower, watching from the street, would not know that the passenger was no longer inside.

Mr. Mount had slept at the Bell Savage Inn, just as he had said. But this morning there had been a flaw in the plan. Somehow his enemies had discovered that he was not at Mr. Cogwell's. They had followed Celia's coach, guessing that it would lead them back to their quarry.

Dick was still puzzling over the matter when they pulled up at the first stage, and Mr. Mount insisted that they should take some refreshment together while the horses were being changed, before going their separate ways.

"Though why *should* we go separate ways?" demanded Celia, catching his arm as he marched into the inn.

"What do you mean, lass?"

"We owe a great deal to Mr. Fazeley, Uncle. His newspaper isn't coming out any more. He is free for the present, he has overtired himself in London—perhaps country air, *Derbyshire* air—"

Mr. Mount stopped and peered down at her, his eyes narrowing cautiously. Then his features relaxed into a smile. He had taken to Fazeley since the change in conversation.

"Ay, lass, that's a capital notion. There's no air like Derbyshire air—an' no fishing like Derbyshire fishing," he added with a good-humored glare in Fazeley's direction. "Let others say what they will."

He was a man of quick decisions. Before the food and drink were on the table, his invitation was issued. Would Mr. Fazeley—and the lad, of course—care to continue the journey with them, and spend a little while as his guests in the Peak?

"We're simple folk up there," he said bluntly. "No fancy manners. You'd have to take us as you found us. But the millhouse is full of empty bedrooms, me having no family, and my housekeeper cooks better than all your fancy foreigners. What d'ye say?"

The little journalist glanced across at Dick.

"Thank you very much, Mr. Mount. It's most handsome of you. I will ask the landlord for pen and paper, so that I can send word to my partner. You perhaps would care to send a note to Mr. Cogwell, to set his mind at rest?"

"Ay, I'll do that."

"Dick and I are used to traveling light," chuckled Fazeley. "We can buy what few necessaries we want as we go."

"I'm so glad, Dick," Celia murmured as the gentlemen scribbled their letters. "You will see 'the wonders of the Peak' after all."

"Maybe Dick'll be able to help you along with your studies," her uncle grunted, without raising his head. "We were talking about a tutor for you. I expect you know French and Latin and all that?"

"A little, sir. I'll help Celia if I can."

"Eh, you can teach her all a girl needs of suchlike things. You look to me a likely lad." He went on writing. Celia and Dick looked at each other across the table and crammed their handkerchiefs into their mouths simultaneously, to prevent an audible explosion of mirth.

Ten minutes later, while their host was settling the bill, Fazeley and Dick had their first chance of a word together.

"What do you make of *this*, Dick? I picked it up off the road. One of those scoundrels dropped it when he ran."

Fazeley produced a short length of cord from his pocket. It was thin but very strong, and woven of fine black silk. He ran it through his fingers, caressingly.

"Do you think they meant to kidnap Mr. Mount, sir? Was it to tie his hands with?"

"Perhaps, Dick—and perhaps not."

"Well, what else—"

"I have accepted this invitation," said Fazeley quickly in a low voice, "not to catch trout but to fish for something bigger. We are up against something very strange and very ugly. I have only once seen a cord like this, in Italy. And it was used for strangling."

Four in a chaise were too many for so long a journey. Fazeley therefore insisted on hiring a horse which Dick and he could ride in turn. But, in the end, the boy did most of the riding.

"It's a good thing to have one of us mounted," said Fazeley thoughtfully.

"I like it, sir, and it's more comfortable for you others."

"It's comfort of mind I'm thinking of."

Dick nodded. "I'm keeping a good lookout."

"Do. We may see no more of Mr. Mount's highwaymen, but we can't be sure."

Each day Fazeley stopped the chaise at some lonely spot and gave him a few minutes' pistol practice, using an old tree or post as target. Celia insisted on trying her hand, and even induced her reluctant uncle to compete.

Neither of them was a very good shot. Dick was better once he had learned the knack. Fazeley was brilliant.

"It is just experience," he murmured casually.

He taught Dick to shoot from the saddle while on the move, to run a few paces and shoot, and to spin round on his heel, firing the instant he saw the target. "Leisurely aiming is no practice at all," he said. "There is never time for it."

"I wish they had Mr. Fazeley to fight the Indians, back home," Celia confided to Dick. "He seems to know the things which *really* matter, not just the rules in the book. *He* wouldn't try to beat the redskins with red coats and pipe-clayed belts!"

"No, I don't suppose he would."

Dick liked Celia, once he had gotten over his shyness. He had never been used to girls, but she was different, somehow. It was not really that she was at all boyish, in spite of her pistol shooting and her air of independence. Her American childhood had given her other qualities too, as well as a fund of memories which he found novel and fascinating. She talked a great deal, but what she had to say was interesting. The long journey might have grown dull without her.

Long it certainly was. Market Milldale was in the mountainous northerly part of Derbyshire, a hundred and fifty miles from London—and the last of those miles over some of the worst roads in the kingdom.

"Pack-horse country," was Fazeley's comment as the hills grew steeper and the track narrower and stonier. And truly, the long strings of laden animals, weaving their way to and fro across the golden-green slopes, were far commoner than wagons or carriages.

"A poor country," Fazeley told Dick privately. "These valleys seem well enough, but the upper parts are nothing more than an awful wilderness."

"You must not let Mr. Mount hear you say that,"

Dick answered with a grin. "I like Derbyshire. It's almost a foreign country—and I've never seen any, as you have."

No sinister happenings interrupted the journey, and on the evening of the fourth day they arrived at Market Milldale.

It was a small, compact town, clustered at the meeting place of two rivers. After the elegance of Abbotsbridge, let alone London, it seemed a poor place. Here were no tall new houses of warm red brick with sash windows and handsome fanlights, plaster pillars and cornices, and similar classical ornaments. Market Milldale was a plain, homespun town, built of the local gray stone. The only attempt at elegance was the small, recently erected Bath House, covering a spring of lukewarm, foul-smelling water, which—vowed Mr. Mount—would settle any ache or pain, no matter how deep-seated in the human system.

"You'll go in a cripple an' come out dancing," he assured Fazeley as they drove past.

"Indeed?" said the journalist cautiously. After trying the waters the next day, he was prepared to believe it.

The larger of the two rivers flowed through a broad green dale, part checkered with enclosed fields, part scrubby with belts of woodland, and part laid out as a setting for the mansion of Lord Lathkill, the local landowner and a great enthusiast for improvements and new fashions. To his generosity—and taste—the town owed the Bath House, which, with its imitation Greek portico, looked as sadly out of place in the bleak flagstoned market square as any nymph set down, shivering, in the Arctic.

"But it's a vast improvement," Mr. Mount insisted. "Place were in a sad state before. Folk came to bathe in waters, but went out muckier than what they went in."

The smaller river came tumbling down a gorge. Here the craggy slopes were given over to hanging curtains of ivy, cushions of moss and beds of wild lilies, and such trees as could find roothold in the crevices.

Mr. Mount's house was the last at this end of the town. Adjoining it was the small mill in which the silk was woven.

As Fazeley handed Celia down from the chaise, and Dick slid wearily from the saddle, the door of the house opened and a wrinkled, rosy-cheeked old woman appeared on the spotless doorstep, wiping her hands on her apron.

"I knew it was the mester!" she screeched amiably. "I've been harkin' for the wheels this week past. Is this your niece then?"

"Ay, this is Miss Celia. This is Mrs. Ruddle, lass. She'll look after you."

"Thought she were a child!" cackled the housekeeper, scanning her with beady but kindly black eyes. "Looks to me more like a young lady. Height o' fashion, too. Huh! I'm sure I don't know, don't know at all. It's not what I've been used to, but we'll have to see. Come on in, love."

"And these two gentlemen will be needing beds—"

"Oh, they will?" Mrs. Ruddle half turned, surveyed Fazeley and Dick over one crooked shoulder, and sniffed. "Huh! I don't know, I'm sure."

"You know now," said Mr. Mount gently but firmly.

"Well, you're the mester, I suppose. . . . We'll have to see. Huh!"

Mrs. Ruddle's bark was much worse than her bite. In a moment she had the maids scurrying in every direction. Soon log fires were crackling in every grate, hot water steamed from every polished can, and crisp sheets of fragrant linen lay smooth across each mountainous feather bed. By the time the travelers met downstairs, the long oak table was heavy with food—fresh grilled trout, cold ham and mutton, eggs, cheese, and a fruit pie.

"It's the best I could do without warnin'," screeched Mrs. Ruddle, as she chased the maids about their duties. "If it's not what ye're used to in London and foreign parts, I can't help that. Ye'll just have to manage."

Dick was late downstairs the next morning. Mr. Mount was breakfasting in the old-fashioned way, standing at the sideboard with a mug of ale and a slab of bread and butter. With him was an old workman, tall but stooping, with snow-white curly hair and eyes of a most piercing blue.

Mr. Mount mumbled an introduction as he ate.

"Will Wirksworth, my foreman . . . an' this is Dick Arlington, who's up for a bit of a visit. Help yourself, Dick."

"Thank you, sir."

"Now, Will, I were tellin' you about my plans for the new mill. What do you think?"

"I think ye're daft, mester," said the foreman.

"Daft? An' why?"

" 'Tis all we can do to keep mill goin' as 'tis. We can weave every inch o' thread we can buy. Where's t' sense in buildin' another big mill?"

Mr. Mount grinned like a schoolboy. He turned to Dick. "Old Will's a proper Peakrill," he observed, taking another pull at his ale.

"Please—what's a Peakrill?"

" 'Tis a miner, hereabouts," said Will. "A lead miner. That were the trade I were brought up to. But then I went for a soldier. Peakrills are always wanted for sappers an' miners—they've got the knack, ye see—"

"And the devilment," interrupted his employer. "They're as obstinate as mules, but if you want some'un for a desperate job, like in a siege on a fortress, you can't beat 'em."

"I were in one siege too many," said Will thoughtfully. "We laid a mine, but we didn't know as there was a countermine. Blown up with gunpowder I were, an' then buried alive for six hours. It unsettled me, ye know," he added without the flicker of a smile. "I quit soldierin' then, an' come home. I didn't seem to fancy the lead minin' any more, so I tried one thing an' another, till I come to work for the mester here, in the silk."

"An' a right good foreman you are, for all you're a

proper old Peakrill," laughed Mr. Mount. "So you think I'm daft, do you?"

"I do. Without ye can reckon on buyin' double the quantity o' thread, there's no sense in makin' another mill to weave it. But maybe that's what ye went to London to do?"

"I didn't," Mr. Mount assured him, clapping him on the shoulder. "Come along out, man, and I'll tell you a word in your ear as we go."

They walked out together just as Mrs. Ruddle came bustling in. Her eyes lighted on Dick as he stood munching his bread and butter, but there was approval in their glance.

"I'm glad there's one of ye eats a Christian breakfast," she cackled. "The mester says I've to mash tea for yon Mr. Fazeley. Tea! An' toast! Next thing, the young lady'll be wantin' cups o' chocolate carried to her in bed, I shouldn't wonder! It's not what I've been used to. Huh!"

She hurried out again, a scrawny, black witchlike creature, vowing vengeance on the maids for some misdeed or other. But when Fazley came down five minutes later, dapper and freshly shaved, to be followed quickly by a sleepy-eyed Celia, the tea and toast were on the table almost before they could pull up their chairs.

Thus began a spell of several weeks which, for those three at least, were unshadowed by care of any kind. In that quiet Derbyshire valley it was hard to believe that the mysterious incidents in London had ever happened.

Mr. Mount left them to their own devices. Apart from an occasional hour's angling with Fazeley, he spent all his time in the mill or prowling around the site of the new one. Life would have been dull for Celia, with no one else to talk to.

Fazeley fished and took the waters. Now and then he hired a chaise and set off with the young people to view some place of interest, and after supper he might join them in a game of cards; otherwise they had to amuse each other.

Celia studied each morning, and Dick tried hard to improve her French and Latin. He felt he owed it to Mr. Mount for his hospitality. But he soon realized that neither Celia nor her uncle took this tutoring very seriously, so he took less trouble to urge her on.

Their friendship made better progress than their studies.

The girl soon laid aside the hoop skirts which, so fashionable in town, were too cumbrous in Derbyshire. In a shorter riding skirt and a wide-cuffed, well-pocketed, mannish coat, with high-heeled slippers exchanged for country shoes, she trudged the moors, scrambled up to high crags or across the boulders of the river bed, and ducked, slid, and swung herself through the darkest and densest and steepest of the hanging woodlands.

It was a wild, weird country behind and above Milldale.

There were pathless wastes where old Will Wirksworth told them never to go—bogs that would swallow horse and rider, or, in another direction, potholes in the dry limestone through which the careless walker might plunge into caves or forgotten lead mines. There were long skylines of saw-edged crags, such as Milldale Edge, where wind and frost and rain had sculptured the rocks into nightmare faces. There was a "shivering mountain," so called because of the landslides which were gradually eating away its westward slope. There were caves, where Fazeley took them with hired guides and candles, in which dripping water turned hats and gloves to stone, and a million stalactites glittered like frost. There were vanishing rivers, which plunged into the earth at one point and came out again a mile or two away.

"It's the kind of country," said Dick delightedly, "where *anything* can happen!" He was not prepared, however, for the next thing which did.

It was dusk. It grew dark earlier now, for September was drawing to an end. The day had been warm, though, and the air was close and heavy in the narrow dale.

Dick was sitting alone in the dining room, writing a letter to Dr. Payton at Abbotsbridge, when Mr. Mount came in from the mill, grunted some remark about the stuffiness of the room, and flung up the window. He called for ale, and one of the maids came running with a tankard.

It was then that the strange thing happened.

From far away, out of the dusk, came a man's voice singing. Dick knew neither the tune nor the words, which seemed to be in some foreign language. It was a gay, casual song—the kind of song that might be sung by sailors or peasants, under a cloudless Mediterranean sky . . . the kind that probably never, from the dawn of time, had been heard in that Derbyshire dale.

A haunting tune, Dick would have called it.

But it is only ghosts that haunt—and the effect on Mr. Mount could not have been greater if a ghost had appeared in the room.

Crash! The pewter tankard fell to the floor, sending a pool of tawny ale creeping across the boards. The maid screamed.

"Oh! Shall I get ye some more, sir?"

Mr. Mount did not answer. She repeated the question. He stood like a statue, gripping the edge of the table. His face had gone pale as cheese. "No, love," he said at last, between clenched teeth.

Dick was on his feet. "Are you all right, sir?"

"Course I'm all right." Mr. Mount pulled himself together. "Shut that window, lad, it's getting cold. And get the doors locked for the night, Jane, if we're all in." Slowly, like a man in a dream, he went out of the room and they heard his heavy tread on the stairs. Dick went and closed the window. Pressing his cheek against the cold glass, he was just in time to catch a glimpse of the unknown singer, a shadow swinging away down the twilit road.

Mr. Mount had recovered somewhat by suppertime, but he had regained the wary look he had worn in London. Dick noticed another thing, too. From that night onward his pocket always showed the bulge of a pistol.

7.   Vengeance From Italy

Why had a scrap of song in some unknown language produced so powerful an effect? Dick dared not ask his host.
But from that evening Mr. Mount was like a man
haunted. Celia noticed the change in him, and Dick
told her then what had happened.

"Maybe it was a gypsy," he said. "They have their
own language that nobody else understands."

"It's strange." She gave a little shiver. "What does
Mr. Fazeley think?"

"I don't know. He just told me to keep my eyes and
ears open."

"There is some danger overhanging Uncle Charles,"
said the girl decisively. "I thought we had left it behind

in London. But now it seems to have followed us here. Oh, I *do* wish he would talk to me—or to Mr. Fazeley, if he thinks I'm not old enough. . . . There must be something that could be done. But how can anyone help if we are all kept in the dark like this?"

"It's a pity," said Dick, choosing his words with tact, "that your uncle is such a very *independent* man."

Celia gave her little gurgling laugh. "Why not say 'pigheaded'? He is, you know. He's a dear, but we're all frightened of him. He's not the sort of man you can *ask* things."

That was true. Mr. Mount minded his own business and liked others to do the same. Even his new mill was surrounded by secrecy. Visitors to the site were quickly sent on their way, no wiser than when they arrived. Questions were discouraged. In some respects the mill was going to be quite different from the one which had so far woven the silk. New machinery was being made in a barn cleared for the purpose. Only a handful of old and trusted workmen were allowed inside.

Dick himself would have very much liked to watch what they were doing. Machinery interested him. Sometimes, when he was sent on an errand into the old mill, he lingered fascinated beside the looms, watching the silken threads woven, by a sort of slow magic, into the patterned fabrics which in time would make a lady's gown, a gentleman's waistcoat, or the cover of a chair.

He was never allowed into the barn, however. The great doors were kept shut. One had to hammer on them, call "Mr. Mount!" or "Will!" and stand there until they were opened. If Mr. Mount had kept all his money in the barn, he could scarcely have taken more care.

On the day after Celia's conversation with Dick, some light was thrown on the mystery in an unexpected way.

Dick walked into the parlor to ask Celia if she would come for a walk. She was sitting at the harpsichord which her uncle had bought for her, picking out a tune and singing to herself in a low, clear voice. He stood in the doorway for a few moments, listening. Then he closed the door and strode across to her.

"You startled me!" she said, stopping abruptly and swinging around on her stool.

"What was that you were singing?" he demanded eagerly.

"That? Oh, something my mother once taught me. An air from an opera—by Scarlatti—"

"I mean, what language? Italian?"

"Yes. It would be. Of course, I don't *know* Italian," she admitted candidly, "but one can learn the words, like a parrot. . . . Why are you looking like that?"

"Sing it again!"

"Why?" she asked suspiciously. "I've half-forgotten it. I wouldn't have sung at all if I'd known you were listening."

"Please, Celia. I have an idea."

She turned on her stool and struck the keys. Shyly, hesitantly, the Scarlatti aria poured from her lips. When it was finished she looked up at him. His face was thoughtful.

"Dick," she said, "that surely wasn't the foreign song the man was singing the other night?"

"No, the tune was quite different. His wasn't opera—it was an ordinary song, like what they'd sing in the fields. But I'm sure it was the same language. Has your uncle ever been to Italy?"

Celia looked surprised. "I don't think so. I don't *know*. His letters were few and far between, and he never told us much. But—" She hesitated, wrinkling her brow. "There was one especially long gap—most of last year and the beginning of this. I know my father was rather concerned."

"He might have been abroad during that time?"

"Yes. And it might have been Italy. All his thread comes from there."

"Yet he never mentioned that he'd been?" said Dick incredulously. Surely a homely fellow like Mr. Mount—a stay-at-home, if ever there was one—would have thought a visit to Italy worth mentioning in a letter?

"I wonder how we could find out? If we laid a sort of trap—"

"A trap?"

"For his own good. How can we help him unless we know what the trouble is? And if he won't tell us, we must try to find out."

So, that evening, when they all went into the parlor after supper, Dick suggested some music, and Celia, with unusual promptitude, sat down and sang the Scarlatti aria.

Dick watched Mr. Mount closely, but he seemed quite unaffected. As the last notes died away, he lifted his head and called across the room: "Very pretty, lass, very pretty. But foreign, wasn't it? Sooner have a good old English ditty any day." He yawned and stretched himself comfortably in his chair before fumbling for his snuffbox.

Very quietly from the shadows, speaking to nobody in particular, Fazeley said: *"Che ore é?"*

Automatically Mr. Mount's hand moved across his waistcoat, hovered for an instant over another pocket, and then resumed its original quest for snuff. "Eh, what's that, Mr. Fazeley?" he asked. "I didn't quite catch."

"I beg your pardon." Fazeley chuckled softly. "I was so carried away by Celia's singing, I dropped into Italian myself."

Mr. Mount uttered a harsh laugh, in which there was no real amusement. "No wonder I didn't catch it. You'll have to speak plain English to *me*."

"You don't know any Italian?" inquired the journalist, accepting a pinch of snuff. "You were never in Italy?"

"Never! Nay, I haven't a word of any foreign lingo. England and English are good enough for me."

"I was asking you the time, having left my watch upstairs."

"The time?" On this occasion Mr. Mount's hand did not hover, but plunged straight into his pocket and pulled out his watch. "Just after seven o'clock," he said more easily.

Celia, at the harpsichord, had not seen that earlier gesture, but Dick's keen eye had missed nothing. His heart gave a tremendous bound. If Fazeley had been in the plot with them he could not have done it better! It was clear that Mr. Mount understood a remark suddenly thrown at him in Italian, though he denied any knowledge of the language.

Dick could scarcely contain himself for the rest of the evening. But at last their host went out to make sure that all was locked up for the night, and there was a chance for the others to compare notes.

"I must plead guilty," said Fazeley with an apologetic smile. "One should not play tricks on one's host, but I must confess, Celia, I was trying to trap your uncle very much as you and Dick were. Your Italian aria gave me just the opening I needed."

"We thought we'd been clever to think of Italy," said the boy. "But you'd had the idea all along?"

"Ever since the strangler's cord we picked up," Fazeley admitted. "And silk is an obvious link with Italy."

"But why the secrecy?" Celia demanded.

Fazeley shook his head. "I cannot imagine, my dear. But for his own sake—and yours—I feel justified in trying to find out."

The next week passed without any fresh incident. Dick and Celia grew tired of discussing the mystery. They could get no further. Then, one golden afternoon in early October, they heard the unknown singer.

They had gone for a walk, and their wanderings had brought them to the high wall of Lathkill Park. Suddenly Dick stopped and touched her arm. *"Listen!"*

On the far side of the wall a man's voice was singing. It was the same haunting tune which had been in Dick's head ever since that evening.

"We must find out who it is," whispered Celia.

Dick nodded. The wall was about seven feet high, and at this point there were woods on both sides. He could swing himself up without much risk of being seen.

Lord Lathkill's mansion and grounds had been the wonder of the county since he had begun work on them twenty years before.

Over all this part of the dale the face of Nature had been changed. Streams had been diverted, hollows turned into lakes, hillocks leveled and others built up elsewhere. Thousands of trees had been planted to form new woodlands and avenues, and an army of gardeners had labored to make a worthy setting for the jewel it-self—an immense palace of white plaster, in classical style, looking from a distance like nothing so much as a giant iced cake.

From his perch on the wall Dick caught only a glimpse of this mansion through the trees. He was far more interested in the immediate foreground, where the figure of the singer was just vanishing down a narrow track.

"We must go after him!" cried Celia, when he bent down to tell her. And before he could argue, she scrambled up beside him.

By this time the mysterious stranger had disappeared, his brown coat blending perfectly with the tree trunks. Celia had scarcely seen him at all. Dick could swear only to his brown coat, medium height, and sallow face. Unless they could find out something more definite, they would be no wiser.

Dick hesitated no longer. He dropped off the wall

and opened his arms to catch Celia as she followed. Then, together, they hurried down the path between the fir trees. "There he is!" he whispered, sighting a black head and brown jacket some distance in front.

"He mustn't see *us!*"

They slipped among the trees in case their quarry should look back. Unfortunately, the dense branches made it much harder to get along. Celia was used to forests and, though hampered by her skirts and long hair, which the branches plucked at like mischievous fingers, she managed to keep up. But they dared not crash their way through too recklessly, and when they reached the sunlit edge of the plantation there was no sign of the stranger.

"What do we do now?" Dick muttered.

He was a little daunted by the magnificence before him.

The grounds stretched to the balustraded terraces of the house itself, which sprawled, with a hundred windows winking back at the sun, beneath a steep ridge dark with woodlands.

The foreground was mainly open. To the left, beyond a chain of small lakes, was the great park of velvety turf, dotted with single trees artistically disposed, and browsed by dappled deer with delicate polished hoofs, as graceful and self-conscious as a *corps de ballet*. To the right, nearer the house, were lawns and gravel paths, arbors and avenues, with flights of marble steps and soaring columns, gigantic stone vases, statues of Roman emperors, and—the special pride of Lord Lathkill

—fountains in the shape of sea-gods and sea horses, dolphins and mermaids, pouring endless jets of water into the lily ponds at their feet.

It had been all very well, in the heat of the moment, to stalk the stranger through his lordship's woods. But Dick hesitated before going further. What aristocratic, disapproving eyes might be watching from one of those tall windows opposite?

"Come on," said Celia impatiently, seizing his wrist.

She was used to the free and easy manners of the Colonies. She had not yet been long enough in England to realize the vast gulf which yawned between their own class and the nobility.

"What if anyone sees us?" Dick muttered unhappily.

"What if they do? Look—there he goes!" She pointed. The stranger was walking across the grass. He reached the corner of a tall hedge of clipped yew and vanished.

"That must be the famous maze." Dick had heard of the Lathkill Maze, designed to outdo the one at Hampton Court.

Celia was already racing across the grass. He could not let her go alone. He ran after her, and reached the shelter of the hedge. It was tall enough to screen them from the mansion. It had no break anywhere along that side.

Celia was like a hound in full cry. She sped along with her dress lifted in both hands. They took the corner together, their hearts thumping with exertion. Four unexpected rustic steps opened before them, twisting down into a sunken dell, shaded by a weeping willow.

Celia tripped, screamed, and flung out her arms. Dick was just in time to save her from a serious fall. As it was, they reeled down the steps together, and collapsed on the leaf-strewn grass at the bottom.

"*Oh!*" she gasped, horrified, as she sat upright.

Of the Italian there was no sign. But they were by no means alone.

On the side adjoining the maze, the steep slope of the dell had been scooped out and reinforced with huge boulders to make one of those artificial caves or grottoes, so fashionable with people of taste. Within the shallow, vaulted shelter thus formed were half a dozen elegant ladies and gentlemen—looking like so many actors and actresses framed in the arch of a theater proscenium. Seated on rocks, on which velvet cushions had been thoughtfully placed, they were drinking pale China tea from cups of eggshell thinness. Now, at the sudden noise, they started up and stared out of their frame, as though interrupted in the middle of their performance.

"What does *this* mean?"

The young couple picked themselves up as a tall, languid figure of quite devastating elegance sauntered forth, quizzing them through an eyeglass as if they were one of the more disgusting types of insect. He was elderly. Under the powdered wig the long sallow face was deeply lined. Everything else—from the froth of lace at the throat to the fashionable high red heels—was exquisite. It could only be Lord Lathkill himself. It was.

Dick bobbed respectfully, Celia curtseyed. Dignity was difficult. Both were so hot and breathless, they resembled kettles just coming to the boil.

"Who are you?"

"I beg pardon, your lordship," Dick gasped. "We're from the Mill House. This is Mr. Mount's niece, and—"

"Ah, *trades*people." The nobleman put infinite scorn into the word. He swung a cane on a long ribbon of lavender silk, as though half minded to apply it to Dick's back, and half reluctant to soil it with such a low contact. "How dare you trespass in my park? Interrupting my picnic—"

"We didn't mean to interrupt you, my lord," said Dick, promptly doing so again. "But we saw a—a suspicious character—"

"And we felt we ought to follow him," said Celia.

"Suspicious?" repeated Lord Lathkill. "In what way?"

"A foreigner, my lord!"

"An Italian—creeping through the woods!"

Lord Lathkill flung up his head and let out an affected little laugh, like the neigh of a horse. He turned to his guests. " 'Pon my soul, ladies, this is vastly diverting —vastly! These young hobbledehoys were in pursuit of a suspicious character, a sinister romantic foreigner, stealing through my woods—"

"But he *was!*" Celia's voice cut defiantly across their tinkling ladylike laughter. "If you don't believe us, look! There he is!"

She pointed. The stranger had appeared again, walk-

ing unconcernedly along the opposite rim of the dell.
He glanced curiously down at the group beneath him
and then, realizing that he had been seen, passed on
without any sign of alarm. In another moment he was
out of sight.

Again Lord Lathkill neighed with amusement. "This
is too delicious! You saw, dear ladies? The innocent
object of their dark suspicions? Poor Foscari, my new
Italian gardener—a capital fellow at cutting a shrub,
but the last man, I vow, when it comes to cutting
throats!" He turned to Dick and Celia again, who were
standing there red-faced and foolish. His expression
changed abruptly. "Be off with you! If you are caught
on my land again, my servants shall deal with you."

"We meant no harm, my lord," said Dick resentfully.
They were not dirt to be spoken to thus. But there was
nothing to do now but withdraw with dignity, showing Lord Lathkill that good manners were not confined
to one class alone. He stood aside for Celia to mount the
steps in front of him, under the drooping branches of
the weeping willow. "We did not mean to interrupt
your picnic," he added.

"But as you have done so, you owe us a little enter-
tainment in return. I have been waiting for a good opportunity to demonstrate how well my weeping willow
. . . weeps."

Something in the old man's mocking tone made Dick
glance up at the tree overhanging the rustic steps. Now,
for the first time, he realized that the willow was not
quite what it seemed. Leaves, branches, and bark looked
completely natural, yet concealed among them he caught

the glint of metal pipes, running like veins to the tip of every limb.

"Come on, Celia," he said quickly, but not quickly enough. Lord Lathkill had stepped back into the grotto. His elegant fingers curled round a stopcock half hidden in the rocky wall. There was a sudden, terrifying hiss, like that of a thousand snakes let loose, and from every branch of the willow an icy stream came down. It was like a silvery curtain—and the two young people were caught, shocked and breathless, in its folds.

It was useless now to think of a dignified withdrawal. Drenched and bedraggled, they went stumbling up the steps, and the neighing laughter followed them out of sight.

Soaked to the skin, and almost steaming with the heat of their rage and humiliation, they lost no time in quitting Lord Lathkill's domain. Their one desire was to get home unnoticed, but they were unlucky. As they trudged the last half mile along the riverbank, they ran into Fazeley, his fishing rod on his shoulder and a cluster of fine trout dangling from his hand.

He paused, stared at the two bedraggled figures, and let out a low chuckle. "What on earth have you two been up to? Have you fallen in the river?"

"No, sir," growled Dick. "It was Lord Lathkill's idea of a joke."

"The silly old fool!" said Celia stormily. "He has a tree all fitted up with hidden water pipes. We were standing under it and he turned the tap on—we were *swamped!*"

Fazeley kept his face straight with an effort. "You'd

better get home quickly and change," he said, falling into step beside them. "How did you come to be there? Were you trespassing?"

"We never meant to, Mr. Fazeley. We were too excited to think about it. We'd been following that man."

"What man, my dear?"

"The man Dick heard singing that night, when Uncle Charles behaved so oddly. He was singing the very same song, so we tracked him through the woods—and then, unfortunately, we ran into Lord Lathkill giving a picnic. But the man *is* an Italian, just as we thought."

"He is?" Fazeley was all alertness.

"Lord Lathkill said he was his new Italian gardener," said Dick. "Foscari, he called him."

"He must be very new," said Celia darkly.

"Why?" Fazeley gave her a keen look.

"Because it is only a month or so since I saw him on Hampstead Heath. He was the leader of the men who attacked us."

"Are you sure? They were all masked."

"I'm sure. I can't forget that face."

Fazeley turned to Dick. "What about you?"

"I couldn't swear to that, sir. But I *have* seen this fellow before."

The journalist stared. "When? Not the other night? You said you only caught a glimpse—"

"No, sir—that night in London, at Wilkins's Coffee House. Do you remember a foreign-looking man, by himself at a table?"

"Why, yes!" cried Fazeley delightedly. " 'Pon my soul,

the whole thing hangs together. I've some news for you, too."

"Oh, what is it?" cried Celia, forgetting her bedraggled state.

"As editor of *The Courier* I had correspondents all over Europe. When I ask questions these gentlemen do their best to find me the answers."

"You mean—you've somebody in Italy who could find out—"

"Somebody who *has* found out," Fazeley corrected her. "I wrote some weeks ago. I fear that your uncle would be extremely provoked if he knew, and I must beg you to say nothing—"

"Never fear!" Celia assured him. "Do tell us—*what* has been found out?"

"I had a letter today. Last year, and early this year, there was a strange Englishman wandering alone through Piedmont. He was not like the English gentlemen who make the Grand Tour and visit the 'monuments of classical antiquity.'" Fazeley brought out the phrase with a tinge of amusement in his voice. "True, this man made some pretense of interest in such things, but it became evident that he thought more of mills than monuments—the celebrated silk mills of Piedmont."

"That's where all the thread comes from," broke in Dick. "Will told me. There's one of the processes—the silk *throwing*, they call it—which no one else knows how to do."

"It must have been Uncle Charles," said the girl.

"That was the time when we had no letters from him."

"My correspondent told me a little more," continued Fazeley patiently. "The strange Englishman got into some kind of trouble—he cannot discover what—and had to leave the country in a hurry. Indeed, he appeared suddenly in Genoa (my correspondent is a merchant there) and rushed aboard an English ship which was just sailing. Fortunately for him! His departure was watched by a number of Italians on the quay, who were waving . . . knives."

Celia gave a little gasp.

Dick said: "It looks as though some of them followed him to England. One, at least."

"It may be. The long arm of Italian vengeance," mused Fazeley.

"I wonder what Uncle Charles did to vex them so much," Celia speculated. "I'm sure he would not do anything *bad*. I wish I dared ask him, but—"

"Not yet," said Fazeley. "He would regard all this as impertinent interference on my part. He might order me out of the house. And I am particularly anxious to remain a little longer."

"To see what happens?" asked Dick.

"Yes. And perhaps," said Fazeley in a graver tone, "to prevent what *might* happen. Your uncle is in danger, Celia, and we must all be on our guard. At least he is aware of his own danger—he must have recognized that song of Foscari's the other night as one he had often heard in northern Italy. He must guess that someone has tracked him right to Derbyshire. It would be so much easier if he would take us into his confidence, but there . . ."

"Uncle is Uncle, and you can't change him," said Celia. "It would be much worse if you two went away. I should be terrified, staying here alone."

Just then they arrived at the Mill House. Mrs. Ruddle was on her kitchen doorstep, driving off a gypsy woman who had been unwise enough to knock and offer the mixed oddments in her basket.

"Away with ye, ye good-for-nowt Egyptian!" rattled the old housekeeper, brandishing her broom. "There's nowt here for the likes o' you. Nasty, thievin', dirty lot! Get off my clean step afore I lay this broom behind ye—"

The gypsy waited for no more. Seeing no chance of a sale she flung out of the yard, with a defiant toss of her kerchiefed head which set her earrings flashing. Mrs. Ruddle turned her fire on Dick and Celia.

"An' don't you two stand there grinnin'! Heaven bless me, what've ye been up to? Ye've no call, young man, to tak' Miss Celia clamberin' about in the river. Don't ye come treadin' muck into my clean kitchen an' drippin' water everywhere! Straight upstairs, an' change into summat dry, afore ye catch ye deaths o' cold an' I get the two of ye sick on me hands!"

It was impossible to tell her the truth about how they got wet; and, with Mrs. Ruddle in her present mood, it would have been unwise to point out the difficulty of getting upstairs without passing through her kitchen. They scraped their shoes carefully and fled past her on tiptoe, Fazeley pretending almost as much alarm as they did.

The kitchen was fragrant with the most enticing smells and the table was covered with new cakes and tarts and pies, but Mrs. Ruddle took no pity on their longing glances. She shooed them through with a menacing flourish of her broom and banged the door behind them.

"Ye mustn't mind Mrs. Ruddle, Miss Celia," said one of the maids who slipped up to fetch the girl's wet clothes from her bedroom. "She can't abide them gypsies as come sneakin' round the door. 'Twas that put her out of temper."

Celia had never seen a gypsy before and she questioned the maid eagerly. Agnes, always ready for a gossip, lingered in the room while she changed and dressed her hair, telling her stories of charms and spells and kidnapings, and reciting some old verses which, she said, were called *The Gypsies' Song:*

From the famous Peak of Darby,
And the Devil's Hole that's hard by;
Where we yearly make our musters;
There the gypsies throng in clusters.

Be not frightened with our fashion,
Though we seem a tattered nation—
We account our rags our riches,
So our tricks exceed our stitches.

Give us bacon, rinds of walnuts,
Shells of cockles and of small nuts;

Ribbons, bells and saffron linen—
All the world is ours to win in.

"H'm," said Celia, "it goes very well—though some of it doesn't make much sense."

"No, miss, I suppose it doesn't. I've never thought."

"Agnes," said Celia thoughtfully, "it is some while before supper. Those jam tarts Mrs. Ruddle was making—"

"Oh, they're for tomorrow, miss. 'Twould be as much as my place is worth if I were to fetch you one o' those."

"A pity. But never mind."

The thought of those tarts, however, tormented Celia all that evening. She had an impish desire to outwit Mrs. Ruddle. And so, an hour after all had retired to bed, Dick was wakened by the stealthy opening of his door.

He sat up, instantly alert. His first thought was of Foscari. He was surprised when Celia spoke softly from the darkness. "Dick! Are you awake?"

"I am now. What's the matter?"

"Nothing. But I'm hungry. And the larder's full of new jam tarts. I thought perhaps—"

"What about Mrs. Ruddle?"

"It would teach Mother Ruddle a much needed lesson," whispered Celia, perching on the side of the bed. "She treats me as though she *were* my mother. She's only the housekeeper. In a year or two I shall be the lady of the house. Till I get married."

Dick suppressed a laugh. Celia's outward self-confidence always tickled him. In reality he knew that,

despite her fine words, Celia was reluctant to go downstairs alone into the dark kitchen at this hour of the
night.

"All right," he whispered. She rustled out onto the
landing, and he pulled on his breeches and groped his
way after her. They dared not light a candle, and there
was no need, for by now they were used to every turn
and stair. Once in the kitchen, they would find a spark
of life in the fire, which was made of peat and never allowed to go out. It would be safe there to light a taper
and explore the larder.

"Wait!"

Dick breathed rather than spoke the word. They had
crept down the stairs, and along the flagged passage to
the kitchen. There was a closed door in front, they
knew. But for one thing they were not prepared: its position was clearly outlined by thin streaks of yellow
light. Who was on the other side?

Celia turned and whispered, her lips warm against
his ear. "I heard Mother Ruddle come to bed. And the
maids. I counted every one."

"Maybe the fire's burned up."

"Ought we to wake Uncle Charles?"

Dick hesitated. Then, creeping forward, he set his eye
to the keyhole. And, without further hesitation, flung
open the door. "What are you doing here?" he demanded.

The gypsy woman was bending over one of the newly
baked pies. A tiny bottle glinted in her hand. She
looked up as he spoke. Her sallow face was distorted
with hatred.

"Stop that!" he grunted, and plunged round the table to grapple with her.

"Look out!" screamed Celia.

And then, too late to draw back, he saw the long thin dagger flash before his eyes.

8.   A Hunt by Moonlight

There was no time to shield himself from the upraised blade. If he had been alone, Dick's career would have come to a sudden end. Luckily, Celia was quick-witted.

Crash!

Using every ounce of strength, she tipped over the table. The pie shot through the air and struck the gypsy woman's side, exploding over her tattered skirt in a red wet mess of fruit. The edge of the table caught gypsy and Dick alike and sent them staggering.

The dagger plunged, but only tore his sleeve. Before the woman could strike again, Celia rushed to the rescue. She careened into Dick, who was already off his bal-

ance, and they both went over. While they were picking themselves up, the woman scrambled onto the ledge
of the open window and fell, rather than jumped, into
the darkness. By the time they had drawn back the
bolts and flung the door open, she had gone, and not
even a footfall broke the silence of the night.

"Celia! Dick! What's to do down here?"

Mr. Mount appeared, barefoot, in long nightshirt and
a nightcap, pistol in hand. The situation was too serious
for laughter, though the young people smiled at the
memory afterward.

Fazeley was only a few moments later. His cropped
head looked strange without its wig, but, like Dick, he
had paused long enough to tuck his shirt into a pair of
breeches.

Celia and Dick explained quickly what had happened. "H'm," said Fazeley. "There's no doubt how she
got in. This window has been very neatly forced—you
can see the marks, if you look. She went for you with a
knife, did she?"

"It was long, and very thin," said Celia.

"It sounds like an Italian stiletto." The young people
exchanged glances and looked at Mr. Mount. He was
pale and shaken. "Mrs. Ruddle may have something to
say about this floor," said the journalist dryly, looking
down at the shattered pie dish and its contents. "Ah,
is this the bottle?"

"Yes, she was just going to pour it into the pie," said
Dick.

"Then I think Mrs. Ruddle must forgive you the
mess." Fazeley sniffed the splintered bottle neck. "I

don't think any smell or taste would have been noticed amid all the cloves and spices—but no one who ate any of that pie would ever have eaten another."

"It *is* poison?" queried Mr. Mount, sinking into a chair. He looked pale.

"Without a doubt." Fazeley eyed him sternly. "Mr. Mount, what risks you choose to take with your own life are your own business. But is it right, do you think, to expose your niece to them—not to mention your servants and guests?"

"I—I—" The mill owner fumbled for words.

"Don't you think, sir, you might take us into your confidence? Gypsies may sometimes steal, but they do not break into houses and poison people. This is an Italian poison. That woman was an Italian. So was one, at least, of those men at Hampstead—and the silken cord he dropped was the cord of an Italian strangler."

"How much do you know, Fazeley?"

"Not enough to help you as I should like to. I know of your mysterious visit to Italy a little while ago—and I gather it had to end suddenly, at some danger to yourself."

"Ay, I'm lucky to be here."

"But your enemies have followed you. Would it be impertinent to ask why?"

Mr. Mount shook his head. "Nay, you've been good friends to me, you and the boy. I reckon I owe it to you. I'll tell ye the whole story, an' then ye can judge for yeselves."

Dick stirred the peat fire into a bright flame, Mr. Mount slipped away to put on some clothes (and reassure the servants who were twittering together anxiously at the head of the stairs), and Celia decided it would be a good moment to bring out the jam tarts and a decanter of wine. Then, drawing up their stools around the kitchen fire, they listened to her uncle's story.

It was all closely linked with the silk trade.

In recent years people had been using more and more silk. It was needed for almost every article of clothing, men's as well as women's. Velvet, satin, brocade, damask, taffeta—all were variants of silk. People wanted silk for fans and screens and all sorts of furnishings.

There was no limit to the demand, Mr. Mount explained. England had never been so prosperous. It was as though Queen Anne had brought back the golden days of Elizabeth. The war with France was over, and not only was the enemy beaten, but England's ally, Holland—who was also England's most dangerous business rival—was exhausted by the cost of the campaigns. Never had there been a greater chance for the English trader.

"But there's always been a difficulty with silk," he said.

There had been silk weaving in England for hundreds of years, and it had greatly developed since the foreign refugees came over in 1688. But the weavers depended entirely on thread from the throwing mills of Piedmont. And this "throwing"—the twisting and doubling of the raw silk into a substantial yarn—was a trade secret, jealously guarded by the Italians.

"They've a monopoly," growled Mr. Mount. "They can name their price—and we're at their mercy. But, with the demand for silk that's growin' up now, they'll not be able to meet it. So, look at it this way, either the world goes short o' silk, or some'un else must buckle to an' learn how to throw the thread."

"I don't think the Piedmont people are fair," said Celia, pouting. "It seems a dog-in-the-manger attitude to me."

"All's fair in trade, same as love an' war," chuckled her uncle grimly. "Well, I reckoned the Italians 'ud never learn me nor any other Englishman how to do it, so there was only one other way—go and find out for myself. So I did."

It was a strange story he unfolded. He had spent eight patient months wandering through the Italian mill towns, picking up scraps of information. Entrance to the mills was forbidden to strangers, but he had managed, by bribing some of the workmen, to get inside during the night. The machinery was most complicated. One or two visits had not been nearly enough to grasp the workings of it. He had had to go again and again, each time memorizing some fresh detail, and setting it down in notes and diagrams afterward. At last, just when his information was complete, his identity was discovered. He had to flee for his life. It was not the first time that outsiders had tried to learn the secrets of the silk trade, but no one had ever lived to use them. The old mill families of Piedmont were banded together to prevent it.

"But I thought I were all right, when I got to England," he said. " 'Twasn't till that night in London that I realized they'd come after me."

He had been in London to raise capital for his new mill. The city bankers and merchants were delighted with the idea of a throwing mill in Derbyshire, and the necessary loan had been quickly promised for the building of the mill and its machinery. But, in the nick of time, Mr. Mount had realized that Foscari was on his trail. He had played his trick with the sedan in the hope of eluding him and getting home to Milldale unobserved.

"He clearly knows too much about you for that," said Fazeley. "Signor Foscari seems a persistent gentleman. He has his accomplices, as we've seen, and no doubt he has ample money at his disposal."

"Oh, ample," growled Mr. Mount. "The whole trade in Piedmont may be linked together in this. They're set on murderin' me before the mill's ready. But they'll not."

"I sincerely trust not," agreed Fazeley, studying his fingernails.

"Is there nobody you can tell, sir?" Dick asked.

"Market Milldale has a watchman," said Mr. Mount with another grim chuckle. "He blows a horn at sunset, an' he calls the hours durin' the night—but he's not fit for aught else."

"What about the magistrates?"

"They'd be all right when the damage were done! But what can they do now? We might charge that woman—if we ever clap eyes on her again, which I doubt. We've no evidence against Foscari. Nay," concluded Celia's uncle, "a man must look after himself and his own affairs. I'm right sorry I brought you folk into my dangers. If ye think I oughtn't to keep the lass here, I'll pack her off to one o' them boarding schools till it's all blown over."

"Oh, no!" Celia protested.

"And as for you and the lad, Fazeley, if ye'd sooner get back to London, I'll think no worse of ye."

Fazeley gave Dick an inquiring glance. The boy's look left him in no doubt. "I think, Mr. Mount," he answered dryly, "you will have us on your hands for a little longer."

After that night, though the life of the mill and the house continued outwardly normal, they felt as though they were in a state of siege.

Dick and the men carried pistols at all times. Loaded sporting guns stood ready in different corners of the house—to the perpetual horror of Agnes and Jane, who had strict orders not to sweep or dust anywhere near them. Fazeley refused to give up his solitary fishing, but none of the other three went out alone.

"I'm the one they're after," said Mr. Mount. "Though judgin' by yon woman wi' the poison, t' other night, they're not that particular!"

His danger was clearly the greatest. The death of the others was of no advantage to the Italians. Fazeley therefore insisted on setting to work and making his host's bedroom a kind of inner stronghold of the house. Bolts and bars were fixed, and the bed was moved into a corner so that it could not be shot at from outside the window. Ingenious wires were arranged, so that anyone trying to break in would set bells tinkling.

Mr. Mount was inclined to laugh at these precautions which made him, he said, feel like a captive animal in a menagerie. As the days passed, and nothing happened, he got back much of his old bluff confidence.

The new mill occupied all his thoughts. Grappling from hour to hour with all manner of fascinating technical problems, he had little time to think about the sleeping dogs of Italian vengeance. The new machinery was being shifted, part by part, into the building. The one giant water wheel was in position. In a very brief time now, Mount's Mill would be turning out the first silk thread ever thrown in England.

One cannot live forever at the highest pitch of alertness. Even Dick and Celia found that. For the first few days they thought only of Foscari and his accomplices, started at every shadow, and could settle to none of their usual amusements. Then, by degrees, normality crept back. They began to enjoy Mrs. Ruddle's cooking again, and slept soundly from the time their heads touched their pillows.

Until one night. . . .

Dick never knew what it was that roused him. Suddenly he was wide awake. Lying in his simple, uncurtained bed, he saw something which must have been hidden from the others in their more grandly furnished rooms. The ceiling had turned red. It was flickering, now bright, now dim. The red light ebbed and flowed like the shallow water at the edge of the sea.

He did not waste a moment. Flinging back the bedclothes he bellowed for the whole house to hear:

"*Fire!*"

Dick's first thought was that the Mill House itself was on fire, but a glance through the window showed that the red glare was coming from the direction of the new buildings.

His shouting roused the whole household, and they poured out into the yard. Mr. Mount was surprisingly calm. A quick glance told him that the fire, though making a great deal of flame and smoke, had not yet gained a serious hold on the building. The strong oaken doors had defied all efforts to force them, so that the unknown fire-raisers had had to content themselves with heaping wood and straw against them and setting light to the pile.

As a result, the doors were now blazing fiercely. In a few more minutes the flames would have spread to the beams and floor boards of the upper story. Once the framework of beams went, the stone walls and the half-finished roof would collapse upon the machinery within, and the patient planning and work of months would be destroyed in an hour. But there was still time to prevent that.

"Buckets!" roared Mr. Mount. "Find every bucket ye can, and dip it in the river!"

He himself seized a long rake and began feverishly pulling away the loose wood and straw. Will Wirksworth and several of the other men came running from their cottages farther down the road. But there were not enough hands, nor enough buckets, to make a continuous chain from the milldam.

"Here, Dick!" panted Mr. Mount, grabbing his shoulder with a smoke-blackened hand. "Run an' rouse the neighbors, there's a good lad. Run to the church an' get folks on the job, quick as ye can."

Dick needed no further instructions. Here, as at Abbotsbridge and in most towns, the parish church was the rallying point in emergencies, and all the fire-fighting equipment was kept there. He bolted down the road, bawling: "Fire! Fire at Mount's Mill!" It was a moonlit night so that the road was plain before his feet, even when the glow of the flames paled behind him.

Market Milldale had suffered a disastrous fire two generations earlier, when a third of the town had been burned down. The memory lingered. Folks were prompt to turn out at Dick's summons, and he found the church well stocked with equipment. There were a couple of dozen leather buckets, five ladders, three fire hooks on chains for pulling aside blazing wreckage, and—the pride of Market Milldale—a brass fire engine with a leather hose pipe.

Within a few minutes this had been trundled up the lane to the mill, pushed and pulled by as many willing hands as could get a grip on it. Other people seized on the rest of the appliances. The moonlit road became a river of bobbing figures, pale and white in their shirt sleeves. By the time Dick got back to the mill enough volunteers had arrived ahead of him to form a human chain from mill pool to blazing doorway.

Splosh!

Pail after pail of water was shot into the flames. Each time there was a prodigious hiss, as from a wounded dragon. The flames would waver—a patch of charred blackness would show, for an instant, like a rotten tooth in the dragon's jaws—and then the fire would rally. There would be an angry spitting and crackling, a triumphant roar of hot air, and then the next pail would be emptied.

When the engine arrived, the dragon's defeat became certain. Mr. Mount paused to mop his glistening forehead.

"Good lads!" he gasped. "Just in time! It's cost me a good pair o' oak doors, but I reckon there's naught else taken much harm."

Dick, too, was glad to pause and get his breath. He had scarcely done so, however, before Fazeley's hand was clapped on his shoulder. He turned around. The dapper little journalist was for once disheveled and grimy.

"Yes, sir?" He followed his master out of the crowd. They stood in the shadow of the mill building, where neither the moonbeams nor the firelight fell.

"There's a man in the bushes, just above the dam," Fazeley said in a low voice. "I *think* it's Foscari. But you can identify him better than I can—if only we can lay hands on him."

Fazeley made his plans quickly. Foscari, or whoever it was, must be seized at all costs. Mill-burning, even without attempted murder, was a serious offense. If Foscari could be convicted of that, he would give no further trouble.

"But he may not let himself be taken easily," said Fazeley grimly. "I'm going to collect some of the younger men."

Without fuss, he picked his men and explained the situation. "All clear on what you have to do? I want you to spread out in a line through the wood, draw a cordon right across from the end of the lane to the riverbank, and then tighten it slowly. Walk back toward the mill, closing in the whole time."

"Leave it to us, mester. We'll get 'im."

The glow of the fire had gone, but the moonlight poured down into the dale, silvering the gray-green roofs and turning the river, here deep and still and placid because of the dam, to a sheet of looking glass. Round the burned-out doorway stood a noisy crowd. Mr. Mount could be heard bidding Mrs. Ruddle bring out ale for the helpers. But in the woodland bordering the river all was dark and shadowy and silent.

Had Foscari already made his escape in those precious minutes while Fazeley had been gathering his forces? Well, they would soon know, Dick told himself as he crept forward with a fluttery sensation in his stomach.

Step by step the party closed in. It was impossible to be completely silent. The ground was too irregular, the undergrowth too dense. They could only hope that Foscari, if still there, was too intent on the figures around the mill to notice any slight noises behind him.

Suddenly there was a scuffling sound to the right of the advancing line.

"Stop him!"

"There he goes!"

Crack! Cra-crack! There were three shots in rapid succession. Then a splash, the scraping and sliding of hurried feet over boulders, another splash. . . .

"I saw him, mester!" cried one excited voice. "Gone across river, he has—way up dale, I reckon!"

Like a pack of otterhounds, the men went splashing through the shallows, bounding over the huge boulders which littered the river bed.

"There he goes!"

"Doublin' back, mester!"

Dick himself caught a glimpse of someone flitting along the opposite bank. He went hurtling across in pursuit. He felt sure that Foscari would never make it upriver into the unknown wilderness. He would break back by the paths he knew, cross the wooded shoulder of the hill, and go to earth at Lathkill House.

Luckily Dick too knew those paths through the wood. He remembered the one he had followed that afternoon with Celia. "This way, sir!" he sang out over his shoulder. And he heard Fazeley gasp and groan: "Follow the boy—follow the boy! I'm coming as fast as I can."

Dick was over the stream by now. His guess had been right. Their quarry was running straight for Lathkill Park. Twice Dick caught sight of a living shadow amid the checkerwork of light and dark. He plodded on, his own breath torn from him in long gasping sobs. He thought no more of danger. His blood was up. The Italian was not going to get away. . . .

This was the place where he and Celia had been. . . . These were the very bramble clumps, round, like immense hedgehogs crouched on the moon-drenched grass. And, yes! There was the dim gray face of the park wall.

He heard the creak of a door opening and shutting, the click of a lock. There must be a door somewhere near, to which Foscari, as his lordship's landscape gardener, possessed a key. But if Foscari thought he could slip away through a hole in the wall, he was much mistaken!

Dick reached the wall. He glanced back, and was relieved to see two of the younger workmen not fifty yards behind. Setting his toes in a crevice of the stonework, he heaved himself up.

On the other side, leaning against the wall and breathing heavily, was Foscari. He glanced up as Dick's shoes scraped the stonework.

For the first time since that night in Wilkins's Coffee House, Dick had a clear view of him. The sallow face, paper pale in the moonlight, was sharp—like the head of an eagle, it was at once handsome and cruel. Foscari was not old. Thirty, perhaps.

His eyes flashed as he looked up. His hand went to his belt. Dick saw the thin blade of a stiletto just in time, and did not jump to the ground. Instead, he drew his pistol.

"Put down that knife!"

The Italian laughed. Barely twenty paces lay between them, but he knew—and Dick knew—the uncertainty of a shot, especially when fired by an inexperienced and breathless boy. Once the pistol was discharged, Dick would be defenseless against the stiletto.

For a moment or two they faced each other like that, neither willing to retreat, neither daring to attack. Then, as the rest of the hunt could be heard close behind, Foscari turned and ran into the trees. Dick aimed low, hoping to hit him in the leg, and pressed the trigger. There was a bang, a flash, and a gush of foul smoke, and chips flew from a nearby tree trunk, but the Italian ran on.

The shot, echoing through those silent woodlands, was like a hunting horn rallying the pack. Looking back before he dropped from the wall, Dick saw half a dozen figures racing to his aid.

"Come on!" he yelled. "He's not far ahead!"

He plunged into the trees and struck the same long straight path which he had followed that afternoon with Celia. Sure enough, Foscari was running toward the open park and the house beyond. This time he knew he was being followed. He was running like a deer—and, like so many hounds, Dick and the others streaked after him.

The woods ended. There lay the park, the huge pillared mansion with its plaster softly gleaming in the moon and its myriad windows like polished mirrors. And there, low, dark, and trim, were the close-packed hedges of the maze.

Foscari was making for the maze.

Having seen those clipped yew hedges in daylight, Dick knew that no one could slip through them. But he was taking no chances.

"You go left!" he gasped to the man plodding beside him. "I'll go right. Follow me, some of you!"

The hunt fanned out across the grass. This time Foscari headed for the left-hand, nearer angle of the square maze, but Dick judged it better not to change his plan. He made for the other corner. Two men followed him.

Here, darkly shadowed by the fateful willow, lay the dell with its grotto scooped out below the maze. Dick cleared the rustic steps at a couple of bounds, raced across the dell, and up the opposite slope. A few more yards brought him to the next corner. He rounded it at top speed—and came face to face with Foscari, racing down the hedge-side from the opposite direction.

For a moment the Italian came on. Then he slackened speed, spun sideways, and vanished.

There was no doubt where he had gone. When Dick reached the spot he saw that it was the entrance to the maze. A narrow gap in the hedge was flanked by two Greek columns, with statues of Theseus and Ariadne.

And the Minotaur was presumably inside, he reflected with a wry smile. The interior of the maze looked particularly uninviting at that hour of the night. The dense yew hedges went twisting away, impenetrable as walls, making narrow alleys that were full of sinister shadows. Somewhere in that labyrinth lurked Foscari with that wicked dagger of his. Dick suddenly felt less anxious to overtake him.

Fortunately there was no risk of his getting away. The fox had gone to earth. But he could soon be dug out.

Half a dozen men had by now arrived. They were holding a council of war when Fazeley arrived, limping and wheezing but still game. They told him what had happened.

"Good," he said. "You're quite sure he's still inside?"

"Can't help himself, mester," said one of the men. "His lordship's mighty particular about this hedge. 'Twould spoil his fun, like, if folks could push their way through. I know. My uncle works for his lordship."

"H'm. The fellow who tried to burn the mill may be a little more desperate than his lordship's visitors. We had better look around."

Leaving two men to guard the entrance, they patroled the other three sides of the maze, examining every yard of the outside hedge. But there was not a gap through which a child, still less a man, could have squirmed, and not a broken twig suggested that anyone had tried to force an exit.

"It looks as though we've got him," said Fazeley with quiet satisfaction. Posting a man with a gun to watch each of the other three sides, he led the way back to the entrance.

He was just in time to deal with a new situation. Lord Lathkill was advancing from the house, attended by a small army of men equipped with blunderbusses and other weapons.

"Hey, what's going on here? Poachers, thieves? 'Pon my soul, I thought the French were invading us! You there, put down those guns."

"One moment, my lord," interposed Fazeley, as the workmen quailed before the voice of nobility.

"And who are you, sir?" Lord Lathkill was visibly taken aback. He turned to the journalist, looking him up and down with some curiosity.

Fazeley introduced himself and explained their presence in the park at that hour. Lord Lathkill snorted with indignation when he heard of the attempt to burn down the mill.

"Outrageous!" he interrupted. "Fellow must be caught and hanged. Can't have that sort of thing. No man's property would be safe for another moment. What did he look like?"

"Your new Italian landscape gardener," said Fazeley quietly.

"Foscari?" This time the old nobleman's snort of indignation was directed against Fazeley. "Impossible! Why should *he* burn the mill? Must be a mistake."

"That can soon be settled, my lord—when we lay hands on the man." Fazeley glanced up at the sky. The moon was sinking behind the moors, but the eastern sky was slowly turning pale with the approach of dawn. "Have we your permission, my lord, to search the maze?"

"Of course. My men shall help you. *I* will help you," said Lord Lathkill grandly. "No scoundrel shall use Lathkill Park as a bolthole. But this notion about Foscari is absurd. Wilkes!" he called to one of the servants.

"My lord?"

"Go and see if Signor Foscari is in his quarters. No, I don't want him. I just want to make sure he is there."

"Very good, my lord."

"I think," said Fazeley quietly, as the servant hurried off, "that he will have his journey for nothing. We shall find Foscari before he does."

"Nonsense, sir!" Lord Lathkill gave swift orders, pointing this way and that with his stick. Several of his servants were posted to reinforce the men already watching the outside of the maze. He chose three others to accompany him, together with Fazeley and Dick.

"I fancy we shall be enough for your desperado," he said with a sneer. "The maze is a private pleasure of mine—I am not going to give away its secrets to half the people in Milldale."

In the growing daylight he led them through every twist and turning. The maze was so complicated, and the narrow alleys of clipped yew all so much alike, that Dick quickly gave up any attempt to memorize the route. Each time they reached a dead end, one of the men carefully broke off a sprig of yew and laid it on the path. Thus they could be sure that no corner was left unvisited.

In the center there was a domed garden house, six-sided, with Doric pillars, a tiled floor, and seats recessed into the walls of the central structure which upheld the weight of the dome. But the sides of the garden house were open to view, and there was no sign of Foscari.

"Your fellows seem to have been doubly mistaken," said Lord Lathkill. "Looks as though nobody at all came into the maze. Must have run another way, whoever he was."

"But I *saw* him!" burst out Dick. "And it *was* Foscari!"

"I know you," said his lordship. "Got a bee in your bonnet about that poor Italian fellow."

It was daylight by the time they had visited every corner of the maze, and rechecked each false turning to satisfy themselves that not an inch of path had been missed. There were sprigs of yew everywhere. But of the fugitive there was no sign.

When they came out, baffled, the servant Wilkes was standing with those guarding the entrance.

"Beg pardon, my lord. I found Mr. Foscari in bed— sleeping sound."

9. The Mystery of the Maze

How had Foscari contrived to vanish from the maze?

The problem was discussed all the way home to the Mill House, and then—Mr. Mount and Celia joining in—over a leisurely and substantial breakfast. By the end of the meal only Dick still believed that the Italian had even been in the maze at all.

"You *must* have been mistaken," said Celia.

"But I tell you I saw him go in!"

"No one else did."

"No—they hadn't come round the corner then."

"Moonlight's tricky," grunted Mr. Mount. "You fancy things."

"I didn't fancy anything," said Dick stubbornly.

"But they found Foscari in bed," pleaded Fazeley. "Do face the facts. We patroled every yard of those hedges—no one could have wriggled through. There was only the one entrance—and it was never unwatched from the moment you thought Foscari went in."

"He *did*. One moment he was running right at me, and the next he'd slipped sideways, and he was gone."

"But he couldn't have gone into the maze, or you'd have found him there," said Celia impatiently. "Surely you don't believe in magic?"

"This is supposed to be an age of reason," said Fazeley.

"Oh, it's no use arguing with him." The girl tossed her coppery head. "I do like a person to admit that he *may* be wrong."

The conversation ended on a strained note. Dick wandered out of the house unhappily. He had had his tiffs with Celia before, but it was the first time she had ever sided with other people against him. But, whatever they said or thought, he was not going to deny the evidence of his own eyes.

Old Will Wirksworth was sitting out in the yard, eating bread and cheese and keeping a watchful eye on the charred doorway of the new mill. Already the carpenters were removing the damaged woodwork and making temporary doors. From now on, the mill was to be guarded night and day.

"Well, Dick, lad?" The foreman fixed him with his keen blue eyes and beckoned him over. "Yon feller give ye a run for ye money this mornin', eh?"

"Yes, Will. But I nearly caught him."

"So the men told me. Good lad. Queer, the way he give ye all the slip at finish."

"Queer? It was more than queer!" said Dick stormily. And he poured out his story again. Perhaps the old foreman would be more sympathetic.

Will heard him in silence to the end. Then he scratched his snowy curls, considered for a long minute, and said: "Nay, lad, 'twasn't magic. Nor 'twasn't the moonlight, I reckon. Ye *did* see him, like ye said."

"Then how did he get out of the maze again without being seen—and let them find him asleep in his bed?"

Will's eyes grew troubled. "I might guess," he said slowly, "but I don't know as I've any right to say. 'Tis an old promise, ye see."

"An old promise?"

"Ay, twenty year agone. But 'twas never meant as more than a joke, like—and now 'tis become more a matter o' life an' death."

"What *do* you mean?" demanded Dick, utterly puzzled.

The old foreman seemed to come to a sudden decision. "I'll not tell ye in so many words. I'll not tell ye what I swore I'd never tell anyone. But if ye guess aught, from what I *can* tell ye," he added craftily, "then that's no fault o' mine."

"Of course not," Dick agreed with a grin.

Twenty years ago, said Will, he had been home on leave from his army service with the sappers. Lord Lathkill was then starting to lay out his park. There was no maze at that time, but the little garden house was being built.

"Me old uncle was doin' a job for his lordship," continued the foreman. " 'Twas what ye might call a confidential job—'twould ha' spoiled everything if it had been turned over to any Tom, Dick, or Harry. 'Twas one o' his lordship's little jokes, like the maze he planted after, an' yon tree that squirted water over ye t' other day."

"Lord Lathkill has a strong sense of humor," growled Dick. "What was this job you did for him? Or mustn't I ask?"

"Nay, that's what I mustn't say," chuckled Will, shaking his white head. "But 'twas summat no builder or gardener could've tackled. 'Twas work for miners—for proper old Peakrills like me uncle an' me."

"*Miners?*"

"Now, ye mustn't ask me aught more. Me uncle's been dead these twelve years, an' never spoke of it to anyone. And I'll lay that his lordship reckoned on *me* findin' a hero's grave in King William's wars—then his secret would ha' been safer still. And I've said nowt much now," he concluded, "save that them as can put two an' two together may be able to make five!"

Dick knew him too well to ask any more. He went away thoughtfully, so thoughtfully that he never noticed the swish of a skirt around the corner of the house not two yards away.

"What shall we do this afternoon?" Celia inquired brightly, coming upon Dick an hour later in the hall.

"I thought of going for a walk. By myself," he added. He had not yet forgiven her.

"A walk? On a day like this?" It had turned gray and misty, a sad autumn day. The house itself was dark, but at least there were fragrant slabs of peat burning in every fireplace.

"I like walking in the mist," he said shortly.

The mist was, in fact, heaven-sent. He could not rest until he had tested his new theory, but he needed daylight, and then he might be seen from the mansion. He had no wish for a third encounter with his lordship.

But this afternoon would be perfect. A dank white mist hung everywhere, and the maze would be quite invisible from Lathkill House.

It had been work for miners, Will had said. One of Lord Lathkill's jokes. A secret. What did miners do that gardeners and builders could not? The answer was clear. They were used to tunneling underground.

Will and his uncle had been hired to cut a secret passage. Lord Lathkill's sense of humor again! The nobleman had wanted to mystify people by vanishing from one part of the grounds and reappearing in another. Somehow Foscari had stumbled on the passage.

Of course, there had been no maze when it was dug! It had been easier to plant the hedges afterward. Only the ornamental garden house was under construction at that time.

In the garden house, now at the center of the maze, lay the answer to the riddle of Foscari's disappearance. And I'm going to find it, Dick resolved grimly; then perhaps they'll admit I was right all along.

Celia made no further attempt to thrust her company upon him. She retired to bed in the afternoon, to make up some of the sleep she had lost through the alarms of the previous night. Dick slipped away thankfully, and set off along the now-familiar path through the woods.

He had a considerable shock when, as he dropped lightly down from the park wall, a figure stepped from the dripping fir trees to greet him.

"*Celia!*"

"I'm so thankful you've come," she whispered. "It's so eerie today. No birds. Nothing. Only the mist dripping off the branches." She shivered. "I've been waiting a long time."

"How did you know I would come this way?"

"That was easy. I heard old Will telling you this morning. Dick," she said earnestly, "I *am* sorry for what I said."

"Oh, it was nothing," Dick retorted airily. "I took no notice. Well, as you're here, we might as well do this together." Though he would not have admitted it, he was glad of her company. There *was* something weird about the mist-hung woods this afternoon.

They went forward cautiously, discussing Will's remarks in undertones. Celia agreed that they could have only one meaning.

Over the park the mist was thicker than ever. It came drifting up from the lakes and hung in broad swathes above the grass. They had to find the maze by guesswork, and, when they had walked around it to the entrance, they could see no sign of the great house. A pale, pearl-colored curtain hung between, blotting out everything.

At the entrance to the maze Celia spoke, softly. "What

if we get lost and can't find our way out again?"

Dick had not thought of that. He scratched his head. "We mustn't, that's all."

"Oh, Dick!" she laughed reproachfully. "After making me translate that tiresome Latin—all about *these*." She waved her hand at the two statutes flanking the entrance.

"Theseus and Ariadne? Oh, I see what you mean. Theseus took a ball of thread and tied one end to the entrance, and paid it out yard by yard—"

"Ariadne gave it him," pointed out Celia. Triumphantly she produced a ball of silken thread and fastened the end to the ankle of the sculptured Theseus. Then, unwinding it carefully, she led the way into the maze.

Dick had to admit that she had justified her presence on the expedition. Without that thread he would soon have been badly lost in those winding alleys. As it was, they were always able to retrace their steps without awkward doubts, and mark off each false turning by Lord Lathkill's own system of a broken twig.

Fifteen minutes' methodical searching brought them to the garden house in the middle. "Now for the passage!" Dick muttered.

If indeed it did start from the garden house it could only start from one of two places—some kind of trap door in the floor, or a concealed panel in the thick central column.

The floor did not look promising. It was set with small tiles and, though they paced every inch and listened, they could detect no hollow ring. The center structure was more likely. On each side was a bench of carved stone, wide enough to seat two persons. Above each of these six benches the wall was recessed to provide a flat oblong panel, painted with some scene from classical legend and set in a frame of molded plaster.

They walked round and round, wondering where to start. Then it was Dick's turn to have an inspiration.

One of the painted scenes showed Aeneas descending into the underworld. It would be just like Lord Lathkill to choose that picture to conceal his secret passage. The fastidious nobleman would surely have had everything appropriate?

Dick stood on the stone bench and ran his fingers over the flat wall painting and the molded frame enclosing it. Nothing responded to his pressure. Then he knelt on the tiled floor and examined the underside of the bench, and here he was more fortunate. Hidden underneath, where no one would come upon it by accident, was a small iron lever. He pressed and pushed. It did not move. Then he pulled it toward him, and it moved several inches with a click.

"Look!" cried Celia.

Raising his head, he saw the whole picture of Aeneas in the underworld swing inward, smoothly and silently on some well-oiled mechanism. They peered into the cavity revealed. A spiral staircase filled the whole central pillar, winding down into the earth.

"Come on," said Dick. "I brought candles." And stepping over the bench and through the opening, he led the way down the stairs. Celia followed, and, after finding and testing the lever which worked the panel from the inside, they closed it behind them.

As it proved, candles were unnecessary. The rock passage which they found at the foot of the stairs was dimly lit by overhead shafts at regular intervals. Lord Lathkill would not have wished to depend on candles each time it pleased him to play a disappearing trick.

"But where are the holes?" queried Celia. "I mean, why can't they be seen when people are walking about overhead?"

"We're still beneath the maze, remember. I expect the shafts come out in the midst of the yew trees—when the hedges were planted, they'd be laid out so as to hide them."

"I wonder where it leads to?"

"Not far, if Will and his uncle did the whole work."

"I'm glad," she whispered with a shudder. "I don't think I like being underground. It's a horrid feeling."

It was not long before they turned a corner and found their progress barred by an iron door. Running their fingers over it they could find neither knob nor latch, but the gray light filtering in from overhead was just enough to show them a lever like the one Dick had found in the garden house.

"Steady!" he said, as Celia gripped it. "We don't know what's on the other side."

But she had already pulled the lever. Smoothly and silently the iron door glided to the left. It was daylight beyond, framed in fern and trailing ivy. Stepping through, they found themselves in the shadowiest corner of the grotto, just outside the maze.

"This door shuts itself," murmured Celia admiringly. "Unless we touched something else without realizing."

The iron door had slid shut behind them. It was most cunningly hidden among the tumbled rocks which had been put together to produce that man-made cave. A scrambling, inquisitive child might have discovered it, but never the dainty ladies and gentlemen at his lordship's picnic parties.

It was easy now to see how Foscari, chased into the maze, had slipped straight out again via the secret passage and the grotto, before his pursuers had had time to throw a cordon around the whole area.

"Listen—someone coming!" Dick hissed, and pulled Celia down behind a rock.

He was just in time. Down the rustic steps leading to the dell came three figures—Foscari himself, the supposed gypsy woman they had found that night in the kitchen, and a shambling, uncouth country fellow. Foscari and the woman were talking together in Italian in low vibrant voices. The other man caught Foscari's arm.

"What'ye tellin' 'er?" he demanded.

Foscari shook himself free with a contemptuous movement. "I am telling her she must hide in the maze until tonight. We have taken enough risks."

"An' what about *my* risks? Ye couldn't do a thing without me, a brace o' foreigners such as ye are. How do I know I'm goin' to get me money?"

"Of course you will get your money!" Foscari's dark eyes flashed. "The richest families in my country are leagued together in this. Money is of no consequence—but it is results we pay for. When Mount is dead—"

He never finished. The woman screamed and pointed at where Dick and Celia were crouching. Foscari cursed and whipped out his stiletto. The Englishman drew a pistol.

It was three against two, with a pistol on each side, but Celia was unarmed, whereas even the Italian woman had drawn a knife. They all stood motionless for a few moments, weighing up the odds.

Dick and Celia were trapped in the grotto. Foscari and the others barred their way in front. The door had shut behind them.

Dick covered Foscari with his pistol, judging that the others would wait for a lead from him. Meantime he whispered urgently to the girl at his elbow: "See if you can find how the door opens from this side! We could keep them at bay in the passage."

"I'm looking!" wailed Celia. "There are so many ferns and creepers and—oh, thank heaven, *here's* something!"

She pulled with all her strength. To her dismay, the door did not budge. Instead, there was a sudden hissing as from a nest of snakes, and through the concealed lead pipes, from every branch of the weeping willow, a blinding sheet of icy water descended upon their three enemies.

"Good enough!" cried Dick exultantly. "Come on—run!"

And while Foscari and the others were still staggering and gasping under the deluge, they raced out of the grotto and away to safety.

10. Cauldron Hole

Charles Mount was no great respecter of lords. He always vowed he was the equal of any man in England, titled or otherwise, and that the day would come when the tradesman would be able to buy up the peer.

When Dick and Celia came running home in the clammy dusk, he heard their story and his head went down like a bull's about to charge. He said little that night, but in the morning he came down to breakfast in his best suit, saddled his horse, and rode off to Lathkill House like a gentleman.

"The bird's flown," he announced at dinner, on his return.

"Foscari?" queried Fazeley.

"Ay. His lordship were very high and mighty at first —till he realized I knew all about the passage. Then he sang a different tune. 'Lord Lathkill,' I told him, 'you guessed perfectly well how yon Italian fellow gave us the slip, but you didn't wish to spoil your little joke by telling.' He admitted it—couldn't do aught else. 'There's a law in England,' I told him straight. 'If you harbor this Foscari, you're harboring a mill-burner an' a would-be murderer.' He saw then it were serious. 'What d'ye want me to do, Mr. Mount?' he says, civil enough. So I told him: lay Foscari by the heels while we got a warrant from the magistrates—"

"But Foscari had gone?" interrupted Celia.

"Ay. He were nowhere to be found." Mr. Mount smiled grimly at the memory. "Me lord were more civil than ever then. Protested he'd known nothing about the man, only engaged him a month or two ago. Well, he's gone now," he concluded. "Reckon he saw game were up yesterday, when the youngsters showed up like that. He knows that *we* know a bit too much, and I'll wager we've seen the last of him."

"I hope so indeed," said Fazeley thoughtfully.

They made plenty of inquiries during the next few days, but the Italian had vanished as completely as when the maze had first swallowed him—only it had not done so this time, for Lord Lathkill had promised to take the obvious step of keeping it under observation. He was not going to have this, or any other part of his estate used as a lair by criminals.

There was no news of the woman, either, or of the

English accomplice. From his description, however, Will Wirksworth identified him as a ruffian who had once been the terror of the district, but had of late years found it healthier to live in Sheffield. "He were a lead miner once," said the old foreman scornfully, "but he niver fancied the hard work."

He was inclined to agree with his master that they had seen the last of the trio. If caught and identified, both the Italians stood in danger of the gallows, and the ex-miner Jem Holsworth could not do much by himself.

All the same, though the danger clouds had lifted, precautions were not relaxed. The attempt to burn down the new mill had roused the anger of the men, and there were plenty of volunteers to keep guard at night. An armed watchman, with a mastiff, patroled the buildings outside at frequent intervals, and another man sat by an upstairs window, a gun beside him and a hand bell, ready to rouse the household at the first suspicious incident.

" 'Tis worth while making double sure," Mr. Mount admitted. "New mill starts workin' next week. Shouldn't like aught to go wrong when we're so near."

His eyes burned with enthusiasm. The fulfillment of his dream was in sight. The complicated machinery of the throwing mill was at last almost completed. In a few more days the huge water wheel would begin to turn. The cogs would engage, and slowly but surely the strength of the mountain river would pulse through the man-made veins of the mill. Inch by inch, yard by yard, the silken yarn would come forth—the first ever to be thrown in an English mill.

"And when I have seen that happen," Fazeley insisted with a smile, "I must return to London. I cannot trespass on your hospitality any longer."

"Fiddlesticks, man! If I didn't like your company, I'd ha' sent ye off weeks ago!"

"It will be so dull without you," Celia pleaded.

"Without *me?*" inquired the little journalist dryly.

"Of course."

"I think you will find other means of amusement, my dear. At all events, I must beg you to excuse me. London is in my blood, and though I wander the world I am always drawn back, sooner or later, to Ludgate and the Fleet. Dick must decide for himself, though. I have nothing to offer him. He may prefer to look for work elsewhere."

"We must talk o' that," said Mr. Mount. "Happen he'll not need to look far. I've got him weighed up, and he's a likely lad. An' what's amusing *you*, lass?" he demanded, as Celia choked.

"Oh, nothing, Uncle! I was j-just remembering something I said to him when we first met."

"H'm!" Mr. Mount snorted suspiciously. "Well, I'd best get back to mill. Wasted enough time already!" And he flung out of the room with his usual restless energy.

If her uncle could think of little but his new mill, Celia—now that the threat of the Italians had passed away—had little mind for anything but the first public ball of the season, which was now almost upon them.

A fortnight ago she had fought, and won, her battle

to attend it. Mrs. Ruddle had declared she was far too young. Mr. Mount, caught in a good mood, had said he saw no harm. But he was hanged if *he* was going to dress up and go prancing about like a monkey—and anyhow, wouldn't a young girl need a married lady to look after her?

"Of course," she agreed. "Really, Uncle Charles, it was most inconsiderate of you never to marry. This is just when an aunt would have been useful. But it's of no consequence," she added with a forgiving smile, "because Mrs. Needham has offered to take me in her party, if you agree."

"The Mayor's wife? Has she indeed?" Mr. Mount grinned like a schoolboy. There was a shrewd look in his eyes. "That were mighty thoughtful of Mrs. Needham."

Thoughtful was the word. Mrs. Needham had no daughters who would suffer from the competition of Celia's red-gold hair and milky skin. But she had several growing sons with their way to make in the world, who, in another year or two, would appreciate not only Celia's looks but her position as Mr. Mount's niece. The mill would be a fine inheritance for someone, and, with Mr. Mount a confirmed bachelor, it would most likely come to Celia.

Fazeley and Dick went too. Mrs. Needham could have done without Dick, but Fazeley would lend a London polish to the occasion.

These public dances were new in Market Milldale. They were organized on a subscription basis by the leading tradesmen, but they had soon proved equally popular with the gentry, eager for anything to break the monotony of the dark North Country winter. There had been some awkwardness, last spring, when the ladies of quality complained that their menfolk were dancing too much with the pretty, but common, daughters of shopkeepers. The young gentlemen had been called to heel, and for one painful evening the company had divided like the waters of the Red Sea, the gentlefolk clustering aloofly at one end of the ballroom and ignoring the very existence of the people at the other.

The answer to that behavior had been quick and effective. There had been some girlish tears, some motherly indignation, and a whispered conference between the insulted fathers. The next morning saw great activity in the shops of Market Milldale, and within twenty-four hours all the gentry concerned had received their bills up to date, with a polite request for prompt payment of all money owed for goods supplied. This sudden shower of paper spread more distress than the worst blizzard. Not many of the bills were paid very promptly, but the traders made no further complaint, because the next ball was fully attended and not one of their wives or daughters was left without a partner. The gentry had learned their lesson, and thereafter the assemblies were of the friendliest kind.

Assemblies they might be called, but as yet the town had no assembly rooms, and they had to be held in the hall of the Lathkill Arms, the old coaching inn opposite the Bath House. There were a few local people though, who had traveled in the south, and had brought back word of what Beau Nash was doing at Bath. Market

Milldale might have no such master of the ceremonies, but new ideas were creeping in, and Mrs. Needham assured Fazeley that he would find everything proper and seemly. Swords must be left outside, heavy boots were forbidden in the ballroom, and only the most respectable persons would be admitted.

"Indeed, madam?" said the little journalist urbanely. "Then I count myself prodigiously privileged to be invited."

So the great evening came, with Dick a good deal more nervous than Celia. He had brushed his suit, polished his shoes till the black leather winked as brightly as the metal buckles, and retied his cravat half a dozen times, but he was all too well aware that he cut a modest figure beside Celia, superb in a hoop skirt of honey-gold silk, with her gleaming hair piled high in grown-up style and her gray-green eyes twinkling wickedly over her fan.

"Do I look well?" she inquired demurely.

Dick laughed. "So far as I can see—at this distance! That immense skirt makes you rather unapproachable. You look rather like a bell," he teased her, "with a red-topped handle."

"Pig!" She swiped at him with her fan, but he danced away out of range.

Then the Needhams' coach came to the door and they drove off. "Enjoy yeselves," Mr. Mount called after them indulgently, and, "We will!" promised Celia from the darkness.

"So she should," cackled the old housekeeper with unusual benevolence. "She shouldn't have a care in the world."

Nor had she. If it was an ordeal for Dick, for Celia it was a glorious adventure. She adored every minute of it —every note of the music, every step of the gavotte and the minuet, every bow and smile and compliment from the young men who partnered her.

"Celia seems to have made a powerful impression on the county—or at least on its younger gentlemen," said the journalist, meeting Dick in the crowded doorway halfway through the evening. "If I had danced half as many dances as she has done, I should be too stiff to move tomorrow. Where is she now? Can you see her?"

Dick glanced round. "Not at the moment, sir. I expect even Celia has to sit down and fan herself occasionally!"

Just then Mrs. Needham sailed up like a powerful man-o'-war in costly velvet. "Mr. Fazeley! Mr. Arlington! Have you seen Miss Mount?"

"Not for the past few minutes, ma'am."

"It is really most provoking." The Mayor's wife was struggling between vexation and anxiety to stand well with the Mount household. "She is a dear girl, of course —very young, too, but if she is old enough to come to a ball she is old enough to behave with propriety."

"What has she done, ma'am?" asked Dick, his heart sinking.

Mrs. Needham stared at him as though his question were idiotic. She spoke behind her fan, so that Celia's misdeeds should not be published to the world.

"Must I instruct you, young man," she demanded freezingly, "that when a girl is not dancing, her place is beside the lady who is looking after her? Miss Mount is not dancing this minuet—yet I have not seen her this quarter of an hour."

"Perhaps," said Fazeley mildly, "she is in the ladies' retiring room?"

"I have been there. She is not."

Fazeley looked grave. "No doubt there must be some quite simple explanation, ma'am. Perhaps she has turned faint with the heat—her partner may have taken her out into the fresh air."

"Very possible!" said Mrs. Needham with a sniff.

"Dick and I will step outside and see. Come along, Dick." And they edged their way out into the dark courtyard of the inn. The cold night was like a slap in the face.

There was no sign of anybody in the yard. Dick let out a sudden exclamation as his foot caught something and sent it rolling across the cobbles. "What's this?" he grunted, stooping and holding it up in the beam of light slanting from a window. "A shoe? Mr. Fazeley—it's Celia's dancing shoe!"

There was no doubt of it. She had flaunted her new shoes so proudly, both Dick and Fazeley knew exactly what they looked like. But where was Celia? She could not have walked away with only one shoe.

But she could have been carried. . . . The same name sprang to their lips simultaneously: *Foscari!*

A thorough search of the inn yard and its surroundings revealed no further trace of Celia. She had vanished as completely and as mysteriously as Cinderella herself, leaving—like Cinderella—one dancing shoe.

Fazeley led the inquiries, with Mrs. Needham's anxious help. The rumor soon spread around the ballroom that young Miss Mount had disappeared, and there was a rush of volunteers to form a search party.

"Where can we search tonight?" demanded the journalist, with a helpless shrug of his shoulders.

Standing out there in the cold yard they were conscious of the wild hills and the pitch-black night, pressing in upon the town from every side. Celia and her captors might be anywhere. Where, after all, had Foscari and his two accomplices been hiding during these last days? No one knew.

Nor had anyone like them been noticed near the Lathkill Arms that night. They might, nonetheless, have been there. Market Milldale was crowded for the ball. People had driven in from miles around. Unfamiliar faces had been common enough—even foreigners were not unknown among the maids and valets and the hired musicians, and most of the coachmen and grooms had been so muffled up against the cold that they were unrecognizable.

Only one point could be cleared up. To reach the retiring room, Celia would have had to go down a long, dimly lit passage, with two doorways opening upon the yard. Given the luck to catch her there alone, the Italians could have spirited her away in a few moments.

"Isn't there *anything* we can do?" Dick demanded feverishly.

"Not till daylight," said Fazeley. "By tomorrow, too, Foscari may have given us another clue."

"How?"

"Celia is of no use as a hostage unless he bargains with her uncle. He will have to communicate with us in some way."

Fazeley's forecast was right. One of the millworkers, coming up the road in the dawnlight, found a paper nailed to a tree, and brought it straight to Mr. Mount. It bore these words: "*Stop work on your new machinery or you will never again see the little signorina alive. When I know that you have done this, I will arrange terms for a proper settlement.*" It was not signed. There was no need. Reading it, they could almost hear Foscari's voice.

Mr. Mount uttered a choking sound, half rage and half despair. Then he called to Will Wirksworth. "Stand the men off," he growled. "No work on the new mill till I give the word."

Dick looked gloomily at Fazeley. "I don't think much of this as a clue," he said.

Celia came to her senses with a slight headache and a dull roaring in her ears. She groaned and stretched herself, and opened her eyes. There was a flickering yellow light nearby. She sat up on one elbow, and as her bare flesh touched the cold rock she was shocked into full wakefulness.

"What has happened? Who are you?" she asked, as she saw the three shadowy figures huddled around the candle. They turned, and one spoke. It was Foscari.

"So you are awake, signorina? You have slept soundly, despite the roughness of the journey!"

She began to remember. She had been flying down

the passage from the ball room. Had she tripped—or had someone caught hold of her? She remembered only strong arms, a threatening voice whispering, "Drink this, you will feel better!" and a cup forced against her lips. Then there had been a cloak muffling her head, the sound of wheels . . .

"I know you," she accused Foscari. "Wait until my uncle hears of this!"

"That is exactly what I intend." The Italian laughed. "Indeed, to hasten matters, I am writing to him."

Celia looked around her. Her head was clearing, but the dull roaring continued. She realized it was caused by falling water and had nothing to do with the drug she had been given. She was in some kind of cave. The flame danced on stalagmites and stalactites of gleaming crystal. The water was one of those underground streams which made their channels through the limestone.

The other two figures were those of the Italian woman and the uncouth Jem Holsworth. They had some food spread in front of them and wine in small leather bottles, from which they filled their cups. It was clear that the trio were comfortably settled in their hiding place.

"Why have you brought me here?" she asked.

"To make the stubborn Englishman more reasonable," said Foscari smoothly. "You perhaps know, signorina? He has learned the secret which for generations, for centuries, has been the secret of my people. He means to open a throwing mill of his own. My sister and I were sent from Italy to prevent him in any way we could. In any way, signorina!"

There was something in the tone of the last phrase which chilled her. But she answered haughtily, resolved that he should not see how frightened she was: "You will never stop my uncle from doing what he has set his mind to do."

"But I think so, signorina." Foscari turned to Jem Holsworth. "You explain to her."

" 'Tes like this, love." The word was fantastic on those lips. "Mebbe ye've heard o' Cauldron Hole? That's where we are now—hundreds o' feet into t' side o' t' moor, not five mile from t' mill 'ouse, though yer uncle 'ud not think to seek ye here, not in a month o' Sundays."

"Well?"

"Hear yon river roaring? It flows reet across t' cave from side to side. Then it leaps eighty feet—that's what ye can hear. It flows out into t' dale, later on. 'Tes the very river as drives yer uncle's mill wheel."

"I've heard about that. But what has this got to do with—"

"This much, love." Holsworth leaned toward her with a brutish grin. "Yer uncle will do as Mr. Foscari says—or he'll never see ye again alive on any road!"

Celia shrank back. "You can't keep me here forever—"

"Nay, we'll send ye back to 'im, all right. Safe an' sound, if 'e's sensible. If not, by way o' the Cauldron!"

"*No!*" Celia had to bite her lips to repress a scream. She saw what he meant. People thrown into the underground river would be swept over the waterfall, down through terrifying passages in the earth, until the cur-

rent delivered them, drowned and battered, at the milldam.

What could she do? It was impossible to fight against
these three. It was true, as Holsworth had said—her
uncle would never find her here. Was there any chance
of creeping away when her captors were off their guard?

That hope was crushed as soon as it was conceived.
The three figures rose to their feet. Foscari lit a second
candle from the one which stood on the rock floor, and,
as he held it high, she saw better where she was.

The cave roof soared out of sight above her head. The
river raced through its narrow channel only a few yards
in front of her, seething and boiling between its crystal
walls. The gulf was perhaps twelve feet across. It was
spanned by two planks, across which the woman walked
gingerly, followed by Holsworth.

"Do not be frightened," said Foscari. "We are not going far away. But you will be less trouble to guard if we
leave you here. The river is too wide to jump, and you
would not wish, I think, to fall in? Look around as much
as you wish—you will find no outlet from this part of the
cave. I will leave you a second candle. There is food if
you are hungry, and wine." He waved hospitably toward
the bottles on the ground.

A sudden inspiration flashed into Celia's mind. It was
a slender chance, but any chance was better than none.
"Leave me paper to write to my uncle!" she begged, letting a note of panic show itself in her voice. "He *must*
give up his plan and get me out of here. He will listen
to me, perhaps, if he will not to you!"

"That is a wise proposal, signorina." Foscari's teeth

flashed in the candlelight. He put down the writing materials he had gathered up. "Tell him you are safe and well treated—but give no indication where you are. Otherwise I shall tear up the letter. Take your time, there is no hurry." He turned and ran lightly across the bridge. When he was safely across, Holsworth pulled in the planks. Celia was marooned. The others moved away out of sight, but she heard their voices faintly in the distance.

There was no time to lose. She took the wine bottles one by one, thanked Providence that they were of leather and not glass, and emptied their contents into the boiling torrent at her feet.

If the mill house had been like a besieged citadel a week or two earlier, that morning found it like a general's headquarters.

The news of Celia's disappearance, and then of Foscari's threatening message, ran through the district and drew all classes together. Volunteers thronged the yard with offers of help. Lord Lathkill himself appeared, leading a small regiment of gamekeepers, gardeners, and indoor servants.

"This is an outrage, sir," he informed the grim-eyed mill owner. "If that scoundrel harms a hair of the girl's head, he will regret the day he was born."

"Ay, me lord, but we must find him first."

"We have plenty of men. We shall comb the district."

"Reckon we'd need the Duke o' Marlborough an' ivery one of his soldiers to do that." Mr. Mount glanced

meaningfully around at the hills. The wilderness
stretched for miles in every direction—woodland and
crag, ruined barn and deserted cottage, cave and lead
mine. Foscari would never have kidnaped Celia without
first preparing a hiding place.

At that moment there was a shout across the yard. Old
Will Wirksworth came running from the direction of
the milldam, waving something in his hand. Heedless of
Lord Lathkill, he burst in upon the group. "See here,
mester!"

"A leather wine bottle!" exclaimed Fazeley.

"Ay—but wi' a note inside it," panted the foreman
triumphantly. "I just seen it bobbin' against the sluice
gates."

Mr. Mount's hands were trembling as he unfolded
the note, read it, and passed it around to the others. It
ran:

*"I am in Cauldron Hole with Foscari, his sister, and
Holsworth. I have three bottles so I am sending this
note in each, and praying that one will reach you by
the river. Be careful. These people are desperate.
Celia."*

"Cauldron Hole?" cried the mill owner. "Thank
heaven! 'Tisn't above five mile from here." He turned
to the foreman. "You can tell us most about it, Will."

"Ay, mester. I know Cauldron Hole. The openin' is
hid among the crags, under Ramstone Edge."

"We must surround it," said Lord Lathkill. "These
scoundrels must not escape. There's no other way they
can slip out?"

"Nay, me lord."

"Then we have them! Rats in a trap!" The old noble-man clapped his hands together delightedly.

" 'Tes none so easy as that, me lord." Will Wirks-worth's brow was furrowed with concern.

"Why not, my man?"

"Cauldron Hole is big enough, but the road in is nar-row. One or two men wi' pistols could hold the passage a long time, I reckon. An' yon villains are desperate."

"Are you afraid?" Lord Lathkill's tone was scornful. "No one is asking *you* to lead the way. There are plenty of these young men ready to risk their lives for this girl. And if they are not," added his lordship, with a deb-onair flourish of his snuffbox, "I will lead the attack my-self."

"Ye mistake me meanin', me lord." Will's blue eyes flashed. He straightened his bent shoulders with an ef-fort and stood up to Lord Lathkill. "I'm as old as you, me lord—I've had me time, an I'd go now, willin', if 'twould save young Miss Celia. But yon villains ha' got Miss Celia, an' that's the root o' t' matter. She's a hos-tage, like."

"That's the danger, I see," broke in Fazeley. "If the entrance to this cavern is so narrow, we cannot be sure of rushing it and taking them by surprise. If it comes to a siege, the girl is still at their mercy. They can bargain with us on their own terms."

"Outrageous!" Lord Lathkill exploded.

"But true, my lord." Fazeley turned to Will. "Are you sure there's no other way in and out of the cave? What about the course of the river?"

"No livin' thing could travel that road," said Will, shaking his head. "There's a waterfall out o' t' cave, to start wi'. River drops eighty foot or more, through a hole in t' cave floor. Hold on, though, sir, I'm just thinkin'. . . ." He scratched his woolly curls in an effort to remember.

"Well?" Mr. Mount prompted him impatiently.

"I mind when I were nobbut a lad," said the old foreman slowly, "there were a dog lost up on Ramstone Crags. Fell down a crack in t' rocks, an' couldn't get out again. I were fond o' that dog an' I were a daft young lad i' them days. So I squeezed meself down t' nick in t' rocks and fetched dog out."

"What is the point of this story?" demanded Lord Lathkill.

"Just this, me lord. Dog were scared, an' at first I had a proper do to catch 'im. He'd run down a passage, so I went after 'im—I could hear 'im whinin', ye see. Well, I hadn't gone above fifty yard when we both fetched up in a biggish cave. 'Twasn't till years after, I knew it had been Cauldron Hole."

"Then," said Fazeley, who had been listening intently, "there is another way we can get in?"

"Nay, sir. I told ye, I were nobbut a lad i' them days. 'Tes too tight a squeeze for a grown man. First t' nick in t' rocks, an' then there were another place down t' passage, where it were all I could do to wriggle through. I could niver do it nowadays."

"But *I* could!"

All eyes turned on Dick. His face was white and tense with excitement.

"You could not deal with these scoundrels alone," objected Lord Lathkill.

"No, sir! But they won't *know* I'm alone. If I take them by surprise from the rear, and then you others make a rush for the ordinary entrance—"

"It is a risk," said Fazeley quietly, "but if the boy is willing to take it, we can hardly refuse. He knows how to use a pistol. And, if we time the operation carefully, Foscari will have us to deal with as well."

In a few minutes their plans were made. Will Wirksworth and Dick, with a couple of armed gamekeepers as escort, set off to find the crack in the rocks on Ramstone Edge. It was reckoned that they would need close to an hour and a half for the five-mile uphill tramp across the moors, especially as they would have to take a slightly roundabout course, to avoid being seen by anyone watching from the main entrance to the cave.

For the same reason, the rest of the party were to be held in the background until the last moment. If another half hour were allowed for Dick to reach the inside of the cave (it should only be a matter of minutes, but there might be unexpected delays, especially in finding the crack in the rocks), the attack could be timed for twelve o'clock precisely.

At that moment Fazeley and Mr. Mount, with a picked body of volunteers, would rush the main entrance. Dick would act, inside the cavern, as he thought best. Mr. Mount loaned him his watch, and he was given a lantern which, owing to the twists in the rock passage, it would be safe to use for all but the last few yards. He took two more pistols besides his own. Once the attack started, there might be no chance to reload.

Will Wirksworth searched his memory, as they trudged across the moor, for every useful detail of that adventure in his boyhood, sixty years before. It was astonishing how much came back to him, and, once they reached Ramstone Crags, he led the way without hesitation to the narrow fissure in the limestone.

It was barely half past eleven, but Dick was eager to go in at once, to make sure that the passage had not become blocked during the intervening years. "But I'll do nothing till twelve," he promised.

"Good luck, lad," said Will huskily.

"I'll be all right." Dick tried to keep his voice steady and confident. Then, having made sure that none of his pistols would go off by accident, he wriggled his way through the crack in the rocks, down into the musty darkness below.

Celia, meanwhile, remained a prisoner in the far corner of the great cavern. The torrent, swirling down its channel, made an impassable barrier across the rock floor. It was too wide to jump, and, whatever its depth, too violent to swim or wade. Anyone entering those frothy waters would have been whipped away in the twinkling of an eye and hurled down the cascade. She had seen what had happened to the leather bottles containing her messages. The memory still made her shudder.

Candle in hand, she had examined the rocky walls behind her. They were sheer and unbroken. Foscari had noticed the light moving to and fro, and had called across jeeringly, above the thunder of the waters, to tell her that she was wasting her time. She was a prisoner there until he chose to replace the planks across the river.

Once he did so, but only to take the letter she had written to her uncle. Back on his own side of the gulf, he had read it carefully to make sure that it contained no clue as to her whereabouts. "Excellent, signorina!" he called, with a mocking bow. "I will transmit it with my next communication to your uncle. It will, I trust, help greatly to persuade him."

Time passed. She had no means of telling how long, save that the first candle burned out, and she lit the second. She sat on the rock, huddled in the blanket they had left her, and prayed that one of the bottles at least had found its way safely down to the mill—and that someone had been curious enough to fish it out. When she could bear the loneliness and suspense no longer she shouted across to the Italian, whom she could see moving about in the gloom: "Is it morning yet? How long have we been here?"

"Oh, yes, signorina! The sun is shining outside. I have just been out to look for our friend Signor Holsworth. He should be back by now, with news of what is happening."

A few more minutes passed. Then heavy footsteps were heard. Celia grew tense. Even Foscari stood in an attitude of acute attention, and she caught the gleam of a pistol in his hand.

But it was Jem Holsworth. He came out of the gloom pale-faced and shouting. Celia caught his words above the roar of the river, and her heart gave a bound.

"We got to get out o' here, Foscari! There's no time to lose, or we'll be surrounded!"

"Surrounded? What do you mean?"

The Italian woman came out of the darkness too, pouring out a flood of questions in her own tongue. But the one-time miner ignored her, and addressed himself to her brother.

"I were near caught meself, comin' back! Half town's out—I tell ye, t' moor's crawling wi' men. An' comin' this way!"

"They cannot know where we are!"

"They know a' reet, mester. An' they'll 'ave us, if we don't shift out o' here—we'll be trapped."

"But where can we go?" demanded Foscari frenziedly.

"Up ower Ramstone Edge. An' then through t' bogs. I know a safe path through t' peat mosses—we can still fox 'em, if we're quick. There's just time to get clear o' cave mouth, afore they're all round us."

"The planks then! Fetch the signorina!"

"Nay, we'll not mak' it if we cumber ourselves wi' her—"

"We take her, I say." Foscari was once more in command of the situation. "Is all our work to be wasted, because of your fears? So long as we have her, we can still win the game."

Sulkily Holsworth helped him to thrust the two planks across the channel. Celia was on her feet again, keyed up with hope. One of her messages must have gotten through, and help was near. If only she could delay Foscari a little longer!

For a moment she considered resistance. Could she push away the planks as the ends were thrust toward her? They looked too massive, especially when Holsworth steadied them with his powerful hands. Better to let them take her willingly as far as the cave mouth. Then would be the time to struggle, when she felt the fresh air on her cheeks again.

"Will you come, signorina—or must we fetch you?" Foscari's cold voice rang through the cavern.

"I will come by myself," she called back haughtily. And gathering up the crumpled skirts of her ball dress, she stepped on to the makeshift bridge.

She was not sorry to be without her shoes, which seemed to have been lost during her kidnaping. She felt safer with her stockinged feet gripping the wood.

Satisfied that she was coming, Foscari hurred after his sister, who had already started for the cave mouth. He called over his shoulder to tell Holsworth to bring the signorina along.

"I'm none so daft," muttered Holsworth. "One woman's enough. If we tak' t' lass as well, we're done for." And with a swift glance to make sure that Foscari was not looking back, he stooped and gripped the right-hand plank.

Halfway across, Celia saw the murder in his eyes. She was just in time to transfer her weight to the other plank as the first went hurtling into the water. For a hideous second she almost lost her balance, but with an effort she recovered it and flung herself to safety.

Safety? Holsworth thrust out a brawny arm and gripped her like a doll. "That'll not help ye," he laughed above the mad bubbling of the river. "Yon Foscari will think ye slipped—"

Crack!

The flash of the pistol was reflected on a thousand crystal stalactites. The echo of the explosion went rolling round the cavern as though in a cauldron indeed.

Holsworth cried out, more in surprise than pain. Celia sprawled sideways, clawing and scrabbling with her fingers against the slippery rock. For the second time she faced the agonizing knowledge that she was falling into the hurly-burly of the waters, but a hand fastened on her dress, stopped that sickening downward slide, and pulled her back to safety. This time it was real safety.

Panicstricken footsteps were fading down the passage to the cave mouth. Dick's voice was panting in her ear: "He's only scratched—I was so afraid of hitting you by mistake. But they'll catch him outside."

Which they did, though Jem Holsworth did not live to stand in the dock for his share in the business, for he died of jail faver while awaiting trial.

The Foscaris had escaped before the rescuers reached the cave mouth. They were never seen again after their figures were sighted racing over the skyline of Ramstone Edge. At first it was thought that, lacking Jem Holsworth's guidance, they had perished in the bogs. But after a few days a report from Hull showed that they had reached the coast and escaped abroad.

"Suppose they came back?" said Celia with a shiver.

"Yes," said Fazeley, looking Mr. Mount straight in the eye. "There is only one thing to do, sir, to lay this bogey forever."

"How d'ye mean, Fazeley?"

"Your life will never be safe while this secret of the silk throwing is locked up in your brain alone. So long as it is, Foscari—or someone else from Italy—will try to destroy you. You can remove that danger in only one way: share your secret."

"Share my secret?" Mr. Mount went red with indignation. "After all the trouble I've had? I'm a man o' business, Fazeley. Yon secret is worth money. D'ye expect me to tell it to every Tom, Dick, and Harry? I'm not as daft."

Fazeley smiled but stood his ground. "You took that secret from the Italians," he said quietly, "because you held it was not right for them to guard it selfishly, keeping up the price of thread to the whole world. Is it any better for you, now, to play dog-in-the-manger to the rest of England?"

For a moment it looked as though Mr. Mount's eyes would pop out of his head. Then, suddenly, his face relaxed and he exploded in a great laugh as gusty as the air of his own moors.

"You win, Fazeley," he cried, thrusting out his hand. "I'll tell 'em. But I've got the start of 'em, and, mark my words, Mount's Mill will throw the *best* silk thread in England, as well as the first!"

And so, when the new mill opened a week later with a mighty waving of banners and blaring of bands, the long-guarded machinery was thrown open to inspection by all the gentry and tradesmen of the district, the first party of visitors being graciously headed by Lord Lathkill himself.

Fazeley was persuaded to remain long enough in Derbyshire to take part in these ceremonies and the banquet which followed. Then, with a promise of generous financial backing for a new magazine he was planning, he took the London coach.

Dick did not go with him. He liked the wild Peak country—after his adventure in Cauldron Hole even Will Wirksworth admitted that he was "a proper Peakrill"—and he saw wonderful possibilities in the expansion of the new silk industry. Mr. Mount offered him a place in the mill and a home until he grew up and married.

"Reckon I can sum up a likely lad when I see one," said the mill owner heartily. "Eh, what's up, Celia lass?"

But Celia could not answer. She was choking with some private cause for amusement, her features hidden in a handkerchief of finest English silk.